MW01632379

I think, therefore I create.

Memories from Another Universe

TABLE OF CONTENTS

The Writings of the Victor Family

This story exists because of a Power. By the pervading energy of the Writings of the Victor Family, these memories from another universe have been (and will be) presented to several dimensions upon lethal rips along the space-time continuum. Presentation of their Truth is the first thing to ever be recorded by mechanically capable beings. These phenomena are beautiful eyeball- and eardrum-bursting disturbances that many may describe as, "bright," and, "loud," upon bestowing their magnificence, if it is not for their timely, unfortunate deaths. Species with histories of and tolerance to radiation exposure, ones who do not comprehend the experience, and those who have become neutral with energy, pose chance at survival. If any are to sustain themselves, they would then face the consequences of this Knowledge. The Victor Family claims no responsibility for any damages to galaxies or ultimate destinies of universes upon delivery of this information.

Structured to be conveniently perceivable, the provided wave of substance is easily deciphered into common language. An immensely complex theory of record, it is read from basic binary progressing through Cryptology. It becomes for many'a planet the acceleration of restoration, peace, betrayal, and destruction, including one in Via Lactea, Earth. American headlines at first called it The Math Equation from Heaven to Restore the Country and the World. In-the-know conspirators, after rolling their eyes at their own state of awe, opened their mouths again to harbor internal mayhem. Later, headlines would read different things.

It begins,

"There crash-landed onto this world an awesome spaceship in the first beginning delivering Victoria and Victor, the Mother and Father. They bore Victor II the Successor and Victoria II the Architect. Then by the energy of the planet Victor and Victoria propagated Brewers, Mercantiles, Shelios and Golds, to be cast aside to breed, live, and work for the good of the Family. The Victor Family is to remain incestuous and not associate sexually with any one lesser. Purpose is preservation of the untainted line of the Great Family. After 333 days and nights the world will be harvested and a new ship will be ready for our descendants in the Thirteenth Generation to continue our legacy in the next beginning."

The entirety of the Writings of the Victor Family may be found elsewhere. They are extensive, and although altogether insightful, extensively boring. It continues, around the end of the preamble,

"These writings are to be preserved of the Family, by the Family, and for the Family alone. They are to be remembered and sustained upon each Thirteenth Generation's destruction of the world. Upon reform new Writings shall be transcribed by the Victors, as this tradition continues eternally."

A mildly interesting segment appears, briefly. It does not give explanation, nor further insight than a warning, "Among the exiles there sleeps a Goodness chosen to interfere, one whom is one with herself; although she stumbles in weakness, she may come to find Power." This is her story.

It is clear upon finding other memories from this universe that the Victors were inconspicuous leaders. As rule and reign were unspecified, no order ordered, people lived, mostly peacefully, hearing no more say than of an old name on the by. A silent Power proved itself proficient. And by the deterioration of Knowledge throughout the generations, this pressure-clogged planet at large hadn't an inkling what the hell was ever happening.

Please consult the glossary for translative associations.

West Southland

Awakening

Noises are in the air, a great movement of people and their things
Distant, also near, and in-between
Clacking and rolling and dropping and stomping
Bartering and babbling and calling and crying
And all of it was there
And there in the void of the air
All of it was separate
Gabriela breathed
Possessed in body
Could hear herself doing it and in her chest she felt it
Suddenly senses became sharp to rough ground
Sighted it wholly happening
All at once
And it seems relevant to mention, also
The dusty taste of the air
And the intoxicating smells of oats, picked crops, seasonings, incenses
A common blend of the world's aromas
Body present to clench aching senses
In a fragile, limited being
Suffocated by feelings, muffling pressure
Gravitated to the world
Flightless

Gabriela choked,
And coughed.

A glint of my eye
Might begin to see
But I cannot

I hold her first
No one nearby
The two of us
Alone with her
Just as my mother before me
Never attached to by another
Only one immediate connection of blood
All others forsaking
Left for deserted
I will not let her be relinquished so
Not my mother's mistakes
Nor mine
I will not let her relinquish me

No one calls her Elle
It is Gabriela, always
A mother's pronunciation
Never a nickname
No abbreviation of which could suffice in her physical regards
Even her Edward, whom she alone dubs Eddy
Does not now shorten her title
No one calls her Elle

Why must we sleep
To rest
To rejuvenate
To regain energy
To remember
Why?
I think Truth is hidden in-between simplistic joy
Sex is naturally pleasing with a complimentary counterpart
The flow of music is easy to hear
Laughter and joy are infectious
And I enjoy the likes of trade and chat
Good acquaintances are beneficial
And to engage a fresh nourishing sense never fails to amuse
Although the unknown grey swirly sky
Ever-rolling and clouding into shapes that tickle me
Is still boring and tiresome to the masses
They are excessively enthralled with all else
Though while all of it semi-entertains
I think my dreams whisper of more

Mother was usually absent, or absent-minded
Though when present she was acutely so
She taught daughter to harvest gold
Chip a bit from rock or dig a shallow hole
Its power carried with
Itty bits and pieces collected
A single shard has no worth
Gold sticks together like magnets
Clinging collectively in a chunk
Detaching easily at one's will
Breaking pieces off for exchange
Travelers know, it and other metals trade well
In some place of elegance and arrogant superiority
There is high demand in Northland for solid minerals
Although no one knows why

Oh, Eddy
To meet someone I adore like this
For no logical reason
I see significance in your eyes
And couldn't tell you why
I crave your distraction from Truth
Your brown hair I must twist into curls

My Gabriela
Worthy to be adored as I do
Logic and reason mean little as if she's found a lost Truth
As if she wants to tell me with no means to communicate
I think she wants what she cannot see
Or Knows, somehow, she can find it
Her wild red mane I'll cafuné into locks until then

It wasn't really red
Or brown, or light
It was, in a way, all of them

This must be why we sleep
For in an instant of waking
I can remember
Dreams are simply honest in their complexity
Everything eases in slumber
Truth is clouded by my senses
This much is certain
It is nearly as though I can see
Without all these things in my way
And I can almost feel beyond the aches of my body
Sensations I might listen to
If the world's energy wasn't so loud

Be watchful
Don't stare
You are distracted
Distracted? I am thinking.
You are not wary!
Why should I be?
The world is a dangerous place.
Gabriela held her tongue
She saw not a reason to worry, as surely her mother did
And thought the physicality distracting.
Be sensitive to your sense of touch
All is warm or cool,
Any may be soft or sharp

Be wary, dear child
Be alert to your sense of taste
For if you should eat something poisonous

You may spit it out right away
Know your limits, my daughter
Recognize with your sense of smell

Remember the beneficial, and the not
Do not make your mistakes twice
Let you know better than me

And do not let your sense of sight
Overwhelm your sense of place
Let wonder not distract you

Let you always see where home is
Hear sense from me, not the madness of others
I inform you now so you know the difference

Believe only what you know, no hearsay of fools
Believe in nothing you know not to be true
And your sense of mind, be with it

It will run amiss and leave you astray
Let wonder not distract you
Let you always see where home is

I want to have a staring contest with the sea
I desire to wander in the woods of Northland
Via a secret staircase one whispered of once
Up the slope from the Käufer road
To meet a merchant with gold like mine
And we will trade just to say we did
I'll talk of clouds and hear fables of imaginary creatures
A walrus, a caterpillar
Unsure why they were made up initially

Conscious to but not a victim of
Maintaining some constant on else's energy levels
Aware, conserved paranoia
One already knows nothing upon meeting newcomers
They may just be looking to trade
Or to take advantage
They may be searching for the deepest most authentic connection
Or the shallowest
Consistently all are on different levels of one plane

Trying to be somewhere I cannot
Trapped in a thought looping two worlds
I cannot see the points connecting
Where I am and where I want to be
In the attempt of abandoning one
Awareness of it peaks
As I quest to find Truth, a Balance,
Naturally I am distraught in this,
An unbearable paradox

Has eternity been forgotten
What verified any of it was real
Were they deceived
Final scene ever-to be announced
Perhaps it was an illusion
Everyone has different attitudes about it all
Which explain their idiosyncrasies
Awake
And recall life as a dream
All in perspective
A journey
Or a timeline
Does it end
Has it begun
Expanding the brink of logic
Does not force answers
Answers are of mind.
Balancing will
And self-control
One could fold their perspectives
Into whatever they wished to see
The Power of determined destiny
Lay in the hands of will and self
How success might prevail
Remains in the eye of the beholder

By whatever means of Goodness
My wondering beauty has been possessed
She's been ever so meticulous
With every thing she does
Bid by her compulsive best
Thoughts never at a loss
And every time her eyes own you
You can see something
Every way she moves
The world moves around her
With every word she speaks
You catch it in her tone
Her innocence is blissful
Her imagination is intelligence
She is perfectly amiss
Driving to madness in search of peace
Wondering why the smilers cry
I believe she is happier than any
Timely progression in her mind
Content behind her compulsions
Something makes a sort of sense to her
As her wonder makes sense to me
I idolize her mind
She is unconcerned of here, detached
So that maybe others, like myself
Might learn to find something else, too

Above, and everywhere, rolled the clouds of gray
Murky and lurking over the earth of the planet
Falling on the sea so far away
The concept of straight up, to the people
A pointless and answerless concern
There must be nothing up there to learn
No one troubled themselves with above
For it was only grey
Obscure in a dreary way
So that no one would care to say
I wonder that we might see more clearly....

Several occurrences upon each first light
With heated energy
A rising verve
Day breaking through people
In summer's happening
It becomes louder
And faster
The fungus, it thrives
As many'a bloem peaking below
From under the surface but budding to sprout
The heated juice pops up and out
All the new patches are starting to grow
A yawn and a stretch
The wanderers, they wake
Or rouse anew their steps
As their pathways take light
And the hills become clear
And the gatherers can properly harvest
The traders and merchants will properly see
The dealings are dealt with most honest simplicity
Foul play and havoc, however, are hardly set aside
Scrounging and professing declaration of, "mine"
And in kind
There is gratefulness
Thankfulness
Hope has refreshed
Whatever had been lost in darkness
May be recovered or replaced
And at best
There is hope
That more will not be lost
As the flip that we flip
Enables a potential for more than less of
What be at cost

Bloem sprouts a top and a stem
Essential entrée
Medicine of mind
Blanketing most areas
Plentiful at its scarcest
It was a world of tops
And people of the tops
Harvested juicy and still freshly warm
Wild growing fungus
Blue, orange
Fat, wobbly
Small, slim, fragile
Hard, rubbery
Black, or white
Wearing personal prints
Each patch exclusive
Every bloem unique
To refresh between indulgences
Realigning mind properly
Maturing bodies progressively
It is how they grow
As if they should already Know
And don't think to
Bloem-based fungus infesting life forms

Basics aside
Crops suffice internal hunger
All together to gain their power
Illinut berries
Fruits from trees of the western Northland
Seeds, and eastern weeds
Or another, never together, (such is poison)
Unamalgamated
Learn, through trial and error
Testing potency in capacity of body
To gain whatever stamina
And, later, sober up on bloem

A black shelio
Resting with a man nearby
Great circles of white fur around her eyes
I have seen her before
With a wild and wandering gray shelio
Shimmering hair
Clouds filtering the unseen come-and-go light
Remind me of its coat when I stare up
Daydreaming of being with my own pet
Or out to sea on my own boat

Draped cloths woven from branches
Stripped thin and sewed or braided together
In ever so small of stitching
Wild like the long manes of hair that grow from the top and back of people's heads and the faces of men
Wild but controlled
Dead and arranged into a dress, cloak, or shawl
Holding onto your body
Hidden cups of fabric to stash a belonging
Carrying this fragment of clothing
Weighted by the substances you fall into
And they cling onto you and follow you
Smallest pieces of energy
In the folds of the spaces between them, the dirt
And your clothes, they are mating
And traveling together
Until some energy or fate or constant tension breaks them apart
But the fibers next to those fibers will always be touching another something
Invisible air latches onto your clothes
Energy travels wherever you go

Lady on the knoll with her trinkets
She's no means of moving
But what good is transport when here lay her possessions
Paranoia protects the tangibly accumulated
Trading fewer and fewer memories
She is trapped here with them
Or lost without
She hoards her life in pieces and things

What is that?

Gabriela watches a small dark figure
Flapping its pace
Gliding, swooping left and right
With grace that mocked a mosquito's misdirected flight
It was larger than the latter by a thousand
And even in this distance
Gabriela could discern a head,
A pointed mouth, and two spindly feet attached to ankles
Below a brown-black wingspan
He flew alone, and cautiously high
Pulling his weight around like he wanted to dive
But dared not

A bird

Her mother speaks simply

Why does it fly so high?

She had to ask this several times
Before her mother would explain
The bird disappeared in the clouds

The feathered beings
Birds used to eat the bugs
Well I reckon they still do
When I was a girl, like you
They flew aplenty in the skies
In any airs, swallowing mosquitoes
So, really, unbothersome
But we shot down the birds
And ate them
And fed them to our shelio
Because the taste of meat is oh, so satisfying
Fuller than fish
Too satisfying to stop after two bites

It is juicy and chewy and an overfilling indulgence....
They are usually small
Never larger than the head of a shelio

She was defensive and Gabriela was skeptical

There seemed to be so many to spare
We kept catching them
And eating them
And feeding them to our shelio
Until eventually
People noticed their decline
We scavenged for them
Feeling lucky upon success
In the darkness of night
A delicacy to our tastes
Soon we were feeling more and more mosquito bites
Slowly we would wholly stop
So when we see a neighbor aiming a rock at one
We aim at him first because,
We are all so sick of being bitten

Gabriela watches where the bird vanished

He's probably hiding in a bush with his mother

She lied

He'll be safe there

Gabriela imagined several hands
Some with knives or rocks or slingshots
All aiming at one poor target
Who must have great cunning and strategy
To outwit several meat-hungry men
Each time it wanted a snack

I used to be the one in one hundred
That believed in magic
Until I realized
I was part of the foolish percentage

Foolish, or hopeful?

To be hopeful is to be foolish
You are smarter than believing in such things

Maybe she should have been
But she was not

We have been blinded by everything
Blinding ourselves from the world we occupy
Blinded by sin, and nothing
And everything

Is there something undisturbed waiting inside
Some eye I cannot now see with?

We all are aware of everyone's flaws,
While generally forgivable, still are regarded with some variance of
Negative connotation

We are all too aware of our own,
For which I cannot forgive myself,
And the people, certainly seem fairly
Self-conscious

And, parallel to the flaws, are
Strengths
Held of some standard importance
In an unorganized society's culture
Strengths do not seem to be recognized as more than ordinary

All is irrational

Sometimes I hold her
Sometimes I see her pretending
And sometimes she just does not want to be held

She cares for her kin
Believes of monumental Good in them
Values the potential of their worth

Trade & Travelers

Energy grows the harvest outward
Take what you will
And trade it
One-for-one
Generally
Unless something special comes along
A rare seed or a complex tool
Or a loyal shelio
With a fair-play working system,
Everyone can benefit
Anyone may go anywhere, do anything
Be anybody

They were all artists
In something that they did
Or something that they longed to do
Farmers, travelers
Traders, and raiders
Creators, musicians
Ones who made
Crop, distance
Hassle and havoc
Artifact, composition
Indulging in passions hardly constitutes as work

Everyone has their initial energy
The time and place
Most do not understand or recognize
The closest to "home" they can be
And if they know it they are that much closer

Forget to act how I want to act
All around me is too distracting
There is little place to process
Survival is time occupying

I have to
Remember
To care not
When did I forget?
I have discovered,
As soon as I remembered initially
We are naturally pulled
Away from improving ourselves
Naturally flawed, or susceptible to flaws
What might draw me in line?

Clean teeth with nails
And nails with nails
Cut nails with teeth
Chew the fat, tear the peel

Faces contort to emotions that have preceded them
A doubtful man's brows are pointed inward, ever-squinting
Joyous people's smiles glow with their high cheekbones
And energy
Is endlessly more sufferable in the lighter

Starting to smell better
Starting to smell a lot worse
Like another person's juice
Or fouled illinut root
Or nice like their berries

When you communicate
What you feel with your words
How you feel with your tone
Why you feel--
That answer is broken
By twitching expressions
You may attempt to disguise your trueness
But energy will always be inferable

Superstitions like shelio shoes carrying some lucky energy
Same reason egos boost embellishment of their goods
It was true that some were fooled into believing
Something has been exaggerated

My services usually require a tip,
Although I'll allow evasion for the sake of spreading knowledge.

Here comes along a John Taleteller this lit day
Who seems to be sure of his good advice
For young girls and their vulnerable mothers
Gabriela listens with distrust and curiosity
Expecting minimally informative rubbish
He addresses the girl and makes eyes at the lady

Do you know honesty, or intention
No
Oh, the misinterpretation
No one reads right
Judging correctly is impossible
Especially regarding yourself

Don't read too much into anything, either
Take nothing too seriously
Because seriously
No one is serious about anything

If this jokester Taleteller was serious, she could not by his own words trust him
Though true curiosity formed her questions
Unbelieving of their answers

I was born, what happens when I die?

He ever so slightly squinted an eye at her
And replied,

One thing that must be understood is absence of death

So when my mother dies
Her body lives on?

The molecules of her body
In this energy do
They will disintegrate, travel, and eventually regroup elsewhere
Kin commonly will, so that both factors may let go,

Burn the body to the clouds
Bury it for the fungus to thrive on
Or send it to sea where it will eventually be swallowed into juice

Will her
Being or soul
Will it have been released from her physicality?
Where does it go?

He squinted now to the clouds,
Then the ground.

I imagine
That depends entirely on her
But I cannot be sure

That understanding lacks everything
What is after life?

I do not know
I only speak of death.

Home is a state of mine
He went on,
Violence is a natural effect
Of competitive nature
And other irrational emotions
He said,
A name is just a title
Association in context
And finally,
Trusting is for lovers and fools, and
Judgments are made by those who don't look at themselves.

He addresses me but talks to my mother
Watery eyes watch him, hypocritically hopeful
I leave them alone
His morality vomit otherwise stays with me,
To some extent

A man of copious travels moves past
Carrying a design of sorts

I half-remember the shape, nearly unfamiliar sewn into fabric
But it's just lines
Some massive, some squiggly
It is just lines into the shape of an unrecalled memory

Many men I meet I mean it
Intending usually upon arrival, your exchanges
Passing on pictures of roads I have charted
Basic beings bargain, but barely
Manifesting model-made mimics of my map
Her air eats it up so passively
Eyes wider than anyone else's, all at once
She looked, she saw, she looked away
Seeing something, or choosing to miss it

I have met and traded maps with many men and women
None of which have surprised my senses such as her
She seemed so interested in the world, yet not the image of it?

In the forests and the meadows
And in the fields of tall grass
Of scrumptious berries and stalks
And fruits the size of rocks
Under waves of power
High in the Northland
Dwell the elevated elite
At home in the trees
A million places to hide
Around them in the land
A million things on which to feast
And a million places to sleep
Gabriela heard say in a different way
That to be lost in the luscious land
Is lonely and unchallenging
Too much too easily
Too nice to visit twice
To farm in the green
Was to sew one's own seed
In the roots of the ground
Freedomless in paradise

In the blackness Gabriela could not see the two men
Their voices were so similar she was unsure who said what.

Mhm
This is some good weed right here
It sure is
Hey, man, where do you get this from?
Old friend back West – travels pretty far north for it
Damn, I feel like dying.
Let's just rest

They lit a fire by glass
Then into it drop their branches and leaves
White-and-purple smoke emerges
Scooping and spinning, slowly swooping the low sky
Engulfing the bodies who lay on the ground
Talkless, with wide and paced breaths

It's good to be sober,

They eventually say,

But always better to be high.

This is the same stuff from before?
Bad taste to it
Never does strike its potency after your time.
What kind of bad is it
The kind of a bad when you start feelin' bad
Or the kind of bad where it's just bad
And you sit in the smoke for hours
And feel nothing
How good can it be
No better than usual
There are always those buds
Do you really want to lose your mind?
No thanks, Max
I'll just kind of lose it.

Gabriela stays away from the strange smoke
A cloud rising gradually in the darkness a short way away
As she curiously squints at their silhouettes
Lying relaxed, dancing only in the airy flicker of flames
She catches a wave of familiar energy
She'd never Known before
A dangerous Truth she might have forgotten
And is surely unaware of now
This intoxication to breathe
Clearly must be more intense than what her mother would suggest
She was afraid to try it, and
Curious.

But she refrains;
What mother says is probably best,
And not as meaningless as she perceives

Young Gabriela ceases her stalking
She leaves the men by their fire
Her questions for now will be unanswered

They were under the impression
They could be comfortable
Being part of a working system
As long as enough of them said yes to dealings
Alas, perhaps the problem was that it wasn't a system at all
But a surplus of little, full-circle, malfunction-prone systems
Doomed to fail when forced to mesh together and navigate like headless shelio
It works well enough, for as long as it needs to
So everyone is comfortable
Everyone is working on it

You build a home, it collapses in on you
It is better to find shelter next to a rock or hill
For those cannot be knocked in to kill you
Or sleep on the ground,
And assume you won't be stepped on.
Those so keen of self-protection
Who build uneasy roofs and shabby walls
Even taking the energy to design
It is foolishness,
Nothing lasts forever.
In a land so full and bustling
Lifestyle revolving around new trade
Slow die men of cowardice
Hiding in boxes,
Never letting go of anything.
Long live sore-footed travelers
Goods brought from farthest lands
Daring thievery, disloyalty, physical pain
Or heartbreak,
Whatever torment life delivers
Wanderers resilient regardless
Overcoming and homefree

There is no escaping
Fear, doubt, loss
Negativity is inevitable
Bad luck will creep behind
And attack when she is least expected
And most is vulnerable
One may prepare themselves
Only to an extent
For the detachment from a known contentment
Most comforting energies hardly last forever
Best is fleeting more often than not
One may never be purely ready for
Experiencing a dose of reality

Something about these walls
Walls of gray sky, walls of growing earth
Walls of ever-over-stretching land
To a healthy flourishing sea
Farther away to see than can naked eyes
Trapped to the floor
Thoughts trying to escape

She carries the gold

Overindulgences
Nice distractions
Complements of self-pity
"Happy on the root"
A bad two-for-one trade
Hard habit
To kick or sustain
Chewing vanity into drunkenness
Illinut roots easiest to come by
Milder than many
But close at hand
Some minds
Too hard to handle
Overdose on juice
Spit the root's shell out
And go loopy for awhile
Until sobered up on bloem
Nuts or seeds to prevent hangovers
Or revitalizing berries
Anything to increase inner energy
Nothing to increase rate of death
Or relapse

Gabriela's mother explains of the terrors
Of insanity
But never the sanity of it

The day lingers on as she grows more sickly
To be burnt to the clouds

And with her passing,

I am no less full without you, mother
Neutral after all
What connection is severed if emotion is absent?
If my attachment was as meaningless as I meant it to be,
What of this relationship with Eddy?
Is there meaning here?
Do I create my own?

And so I call this shelio Pap
We go together
With a certain amount of trust
Whichever road we fancy to stroll
What a bond between such strange creatures
Wanting the world and our company
The world all the while at our feet
Who might be a friendly accomplice
If satisfaction needs less to be full
Warm thoughts surround our being
War of trades and peace are numb to mind
When desire might be lost with honest trust
We can prove to be much too comfortable with a friend
Without concern of misstepping
While dangers are ever as present

Departure

You are not meant to be here forever
All want to stay or go sometimes
But you constantly want both
And you must choose the latter

Nothing to stay for
Stuck around anyway
Made some commitments
Looking for more
And in them, also
A reason to stay
A reason to leave
No prospect of return
No prospect of consequence
Whatever potential
To be had or avoided
And vice versa and all that

You must travel
You must desire to see the world as travelers do
Do not linger here for anyone

That is not the world I desire to see

But Gabriela, that is the world
This is the world
And you're latching onto too little a piece of it

I choose to be here with you

You deserve better,
More than this world can offer
But take as much of it as you can

You are important to me, I want to stay

You must leave me behind
There is no purpose in remaining here
I am not an excuse to stay, but a reason to leave

Don't talk like this

I will not be the one to keep you here
Gabriela, please
This isn't easy

I... won't leave you

You can
You've got to
We can't be together anymore.

Some elixir in their connection; separated between them
Eventually, honestly
She finally turned away
Edward turned his back, too.
When she glanced for a look
He was faced away;
His hair she'd curled her only memory for awhile.
She whistled to Pap and they headed
Northwest

Edward turned round to watch them go
Until she was a dot on the horizon
And for a while after that
Stared in the direction she'd gone
As night fell after her
Hoping, but knowing better
She might return to him

Ways to Edgar Gap

Music

She squints at the sky, just wondering
Until her pupils expand at the drastic fall of black
Tones around ring together
A half a million soloists ensemble
They clamor in the promptly falling night
It brings darkness to the land Gabriela has never walked
Drum circles around fires and strangers around everywhere

Farther north in the West Southland
Landscape littered with rocks and ash
Roads a fine dust of it
She had heard many stories
But until now never seen
Blackness of the place
Never until now heard
Surrounding sound
Inhabitants of these areas pick up rocks
Hit them together
Gangs making beats
Creating something worthwhile
However worthwhile rocks can be
Harmonious noises
Pretty on the ears
Repetitive patterns
In so rock gangs became famous
As the common song goes,
"Poor Dane
Him and John
Didn't get along
He smashed Dane's head between two rocks
To make a pretty song
Don, don, don, Dane
John, don, donk
Poor Dane
Him and John...."
And repeats as such
With whatever curses
And clever phrases the singer can rhyme by

A Noise
On top of ten thousand noises
Thundering from all sides
For a second there is nothing to be heard,
Then everything.

Easily lost in tones of music
They sing to the soul
Simplify the mind
Mystifying sounds
Sending us to sleep

Lose the curl in your hair
March on air
Don't be afraid
To play unfair
Avoid the glare, stare
Lock eyes anywhere
You keep the street
Don't act too rare
Fix both your feet
Find something to eat
Never worry or care
Trades for treat
Control the heat
Be memory that'll fade
And find your beat
Ways of incognito trade

In my homeland there are girls like me
Encounter is unsettling
In uncertainties
I have been here before
But certainly not on this plane
A flash of a dream or a memory
Tied in with some emotion that might be had
In meeting for the first chronological time
This girl, I recognize
With a fantastic energy that shakes me
But her way is enticing
Fantasies out of mind in a trice
I can see terror in her good companionship
And the flash recedes instantly

Women have a certain way
While she is relaxed
Some hidden personal purpose affronts her
Some initial way in which she walks
Is of a predetermined direction

I go with the girl for some time
She is older, not considerably so
We sleep together for safety and deal for pleasure
We sing and rhyme with the air
Curl hair and barter with rocks
In less time than it would take to walk a thousand steps,
We trade off and up
From a pocketful of futile pebbles
To a bushel of berries
And once a useless reckless
Had a pretty feathered necklace
And manifest our best, we did
I fashioned lint from my folds into something witty
She stole the rest
And we indulged in our profits
My memory has been so faded
In these encounters with her

By Amber's future and Gabriela's past
The girls are similar but not alike
Amber keeps a smart distance
Gabriela maintains the same one

Her name is Amber
She carries an oil
She says,
Is from innocuous leaves of Red Orchards
Crimson like the circles around the blackness in her eyes
She is left-handed
Sometimes she pretends not to be
And even in good trust with me
Her lies are strong as her eyes

She called her stuff ROO
She washed her eyes with it
And I handled a few dabs into my hair at her advice
This stuff was good
The taste remaining on my hands
It reminds me of
Blood and trees
Three applications and two sleeps later
It enriched my curls
Twisting their thick shape
Into a shinny, smooth,
And wild mane

I stare into the fire

Why do you watch it burn,

She asks

I don't know.

Amber would not
Or could not
Stop bathing in her oil
Gabriela would not
And could not
Stay around the atrocious aroma.

In lieu of falling southwest with the girl
Gabriela led Pap north, for now

Gabriela knew
When Edward first spoke last
The lies she told him
Would no longer be sufficient
As she wants to find peace
In music, or some rhythm
Stagnancy is paralysis
She travels now
To learn and to find
Unsure of what-
What she might discover
Continuing in a direction
Hoping, perhaps foolishly
To uncover meaning or reason
In their absence she's nothing to lose

Mayhem

While there is music, there is mayhem
Where rocks sit peacefully also violence survives
Only guesses tell where the start is
Bad and Evil people who have become
Who've had things taken, stripped, burned, broken, buried
A life, a means, a quest for happiness: destroyed
To make way for the contagious wrath of misfortunate
Wrapping, squeezing its way around air pipes
Thieves create thieves and murderers, murderers
A vicious cycle
Ever-present
Fear gained
Nothing spared
Strength of hope tested
Suspected initiation from the deepest South and West
So many rocks to throw
Or be hit by
Mayhem covers this land
From every which way
There is no end

Several boulders within range
That rocks have been chipped from
Skteches inscribed in
Graffiti, burns, and other markings
And from this one near I see grow a web
Sprouting out this boulder
Erupting marks in a spindly pattern
Bleeding white lines
On black and blue bloem

Mosquitoes are thick here
Born of bloem in bad energy
They are tiny little bugs
They eat tiny little bits
To enlarge ten times their size
Sprout wings and grow wits
And buzz around to bite and sting
Cause their own panic
And fuck in it

I am tense
Faintly paranoid
Apparently likewise
As everyone around feeds me this
Lost in translation
Unrighteous
Unopposed
Misconceptions
Cause
Are caused by
Themselves
Each communication furthering levels of misunderstanding
Evaporated judgment
Importance unrecognizable
Molecules to never regroup sanely
Basis of intention
Quantity of seriousness
A mystery to all parties

Reigning calamity several thousand steps away
Farther to the south and even more west
Clouds so thick with chaos that acid rained
People of the deep West Southland
Praise their roads
Don't mess with the locals
Everyone else
Says don't bother messing with them

How can one progress
Without a full understanding of current being
False progression is digression
Falling further from ourselves
With every lie we choose to follow
Open your eyes
We are blind
Becoming more distracted
In technology
And in self sorrow

I may not find a home on my road
Even compromising with imperfection
Doubt, here, is such a certainty
Advancing away from familiar
Does not lead day on
Failure is unpreventable
If one does not pursue triumph
Or if fate should not let one have it
I wonder what sort of place I might have.

Hot air of my fingers tangled in shelio fur
This essence is free from hate
Things are simply attracted to each other
Whoever is together and how
Each thing goes with every other
Warming another
Until they are torn
I can't see how reason has anything to do with it

To be impulsive and comfortable
Would go hand in hand, with Edward
There was no disapproval to fear
Here, alone, they contradict
Gabriela believes in her potential Good
And is anxious of the possible result
Wishing to anticipate nothing
By the fear of losing what might be gained

Western Slope

The night washed away with vague memories of Amber and a rough terrain
Her path again became clear by the illumination of Edgar's Gap
And the traffic to and fro the road to Käufer house

Up becomes steep as one travels east
As Edgar's Gap climbs into a mountain
Situational direction, contrasting, "down by the sea"
The land is drier there
One may feel to be a liquid being
Amongst dust so fine
Perhaps they are
In the ways people flow together, that seems possible
Though through my interpretations it is the energy that flows with them

Käufer house
Trade center
West of the river
Just south of the gap
Nearly as far up the slope one could go
The middle of rocky nowhere
A few recent generations of inbreeds
Built a tangible home
Creation unique to the society of the world
The only known building
Incomparable across the land
It had walls,
And windows
Three doors to the inside
A roof;
It was shelter
The Käufers
Famed family of great wealth
Sisters and sons
Exercising legacy
Every commodity imagined
And any one forgot
Frequented by merchants and travelers from afar
Deceitful rumors claim endorsement from the Victors
The independent Käufers created their store from scratch
Smart saving and starving and slaving for their siblings
Inventing a fine edge of trading skills
So that finally they'd preserved enough reserve
To initiate the dawn of monopoly
Their basic harvest entity: skills
Their biggest gain, neither wealth nor respect: power.

Hearing say of wondrous tales
Stories that never cease to give chills
Many of them stay with us
Possibly all of them, somewhere
Haunting our dreams
Crawling up our backs, like an insect
Never the same after our irrelevance appears

From all of the wasted exertion
Who remembers to ask why
No one ever seems to know reason
For all of the gray gassy shapes in the sky

One may never be purely ready
For experiencing a dose of reality

An Account of Victor XIII

As Victor XIII, one born with a number as His purpose, it is regretful to say that the awkward tension of the Thirteenth Siblingship has realistically begun to tear this Family of Power apart. I must say that my respect is in favor of the good of my Family, without exception, so it is with pride and sadness I bear the following truth: Vittorio the Vital, my kin, has done away with the Twelfth Generation.

What's more is my sister seems slightly sympathetic toward the traitor's aims. She is terrified by the treasonous brutal murders of our parents, and I would never mistrust Her to be one to upset our Family's destiny, but I do worry. Victoria's compassion about the lesser men exiled, descendants of ones our ancestors bred to work for our Family in the most recent beginning, pushes belief we are equals. I remind her there is nothing we can do but to fulfill our destinies for the good of our Family. She is unsettled at thought of being a new world's mother, but so valiantly strong-hearted that I never envision her going the way of my treacherous little brother.

Vittorio's betrayal has drained the color from Feli's face. We only ever call Her Feli. She is young, easily frightened, and very timid; very, very quiet. I trust Her loyalty, to myself, and to our Family. She is obedient to me, and loving. She has not left my side since the tragedy. When She weeps She is humble and tries to hide Her sweet sensitivity. I can only hope She will play her part well to save us. She has hardly seen nine full days; twenty less than Victoria, the eldest, who has seen two more than I and twelve more than Vittorio.

All will be how we believe if we continue with our destinies.

Crossing the Gap

Bottom

People's insanity has not wavered in new places
Just the nature of it
I know not what to expect in the luscious Northland
This dryness is deserted as if it meant death
Near the steepest slopes of Victor's Point
Up the western Western Slope
To a quiet rumor of a ladder
Whispered to me once
My secret back-road to bliss
I have come upon it and look, up
Up towards a flourishing land
That I believe to have dreamed of

Her imagination is anticipative
She approaches swiftly
Eyes fixed on what she can't see yet over top

Climb

The stairs ascended
A girl climbed them,
Above Pap, a protective and diligent mountaineer

She wondered,

Sprials and circles of outer space
What are the meanings of these cycles
Why does night come and go
As the light wraps around us so many times
Why do we want to live
To see the end of our days
Why do we sec retly pray
For epic disaster
Does it seem significant enough
To see yourself slaughtered
When your kin is wasted
Your world destroyed
Your love vanished
Limbs burnt
Ears frozen
Body mangled
Spirit suffocated
What then

What do memories mean

Circles and circles of outer space

Top

Clarity
Choosing to ignore how deadly the spot would be to fall from
Such a natural energy sieved through the pores of her skin
Easing up her spine and into her heart
Filling it with peace and excitement
More wonder, a hint of joy
Unknown Good in the mysterious forests in Northland
Hesitationless temerity

I fear my eyes play tricks on me
This surely cannot be the land from my dreams

(And it was not)

And yet I have just climbed a ladder
To place of altitudic beauty and flourishment
These branches beside are roots growing deep through this higher ground
And they are breathing
They are alive
I can feel them in this high air.
Everywhere there is more to see
But all I have anticipated here
Is exactly how I expected, nothing more
My questions are the same
Why are these lands uninfested with wanderers?
People do not wait for openings here
There is no threat in the meantime
No thieves or floating families
Most of the world is condensed to the South
I wonder why, as this land is so plentiful
And their traditions disregarded elsewhere

Northland

Orange Family

According to unwritten custom
This land belonged to someone
Farmers with acres
And several inbred sons
Where Mercantile blood is thick among Brewers
Further north
Still the aroma of haughtiness
Stiffens your senses to the air
Of ownership, pride, and what appeared as peaceful competition
Here is Gabriela, wandering
Through the trees, stepping slowly
And eating everything with her wide eyes
Touching nothing so far but with her feet the fertile soil
Only admiring a wonderland

Ranges of nurseries
In the expanses of land
Fruits by the fields
And trees by the territory
Gardens galore
And pastures aplenty
Quite easy to behave aimlessly
Though Gabriela wandered with purpose
Reading roots for their relevance
Interpreting substance for its sustenance

I believe in heroes from other places
Overwhelmed by their ethical intentions
Travelers, with ultra-natural powers
Secret identities
Spending their time for others
Smiling at people, creating Good
Spitting on the heads of cheaters
Tripping robbers
Causing Evil to stumble
I believe they visit places for short times
Playing their roles, then moving on
People believe they possess Good and Evil
While Good and Evil possess them

I am fortunate to meet the father of the Oranges
Who is welcoming to transients like me
His life turning around cultivation at every dawn
His family, his farm, and his place in the world

A pulpy mess
Tonguing your fingertips
Free from melty, semisweet orange flavor
Eating even the peel and pit
Best not let waste
You swab and swallow
But your saliva is wet and savory;
The taste remains
Your stomach rumbles
Almost as if it acknowledged, already knew
Indulgence creeping toward it
Suddenly your mind seems to turn on to it, too
You widen your gaze
Plainly a placebo effect
So to compromise with reality
You eat some blue delicious bloem
It is as warm as is its aroma
And the watery spongejuice washed the orange down easily
Ridding the sweet,
Enhancing a bitter presence of place
Your stomach rumbles again
Sour aroma, now in the time
Might be counterbalanced by comfortable surrounding energies
But your mind is so distracted you hardly notice
What do you wonder about
Sitting here, in this forest
Thinking about the coming moments
Not knowing really how
No intended direction of contemplation
You'd be right in blindness
The coming magnificence
You sitting there, with thought
Mild anticipation
Not long since will turn to hysteria
Waiting, ego, and mysterious feeling
Cannot ever-latch, cannot stop what will ensue

His boy,
He takes after his father
This prospect is driving him insane
His anger multiplies with age
Taking no responsibility with it
Influenced by passing blame
He is a selfish boy, lazy, full of lies
Unappreciative of life
Self-devaluing
Pity-stricken in misfortune
He is an addict
Either caring too much or too little
His thoughts are direct and actions twisted
Everything is for personal gain
His morality reasonably gone in the passing
He tries to hide his feelings, but
They burst through seams
His head bubbles with hate
His hair and eyes bubble
Never able to restrain himself properly
When he tries to not explode with rage
Nothing's left but an implosion of red-faced tears
When sad, he's fat and lazy and attached to indulging
He moves little and whines much and sighs much
When happy, he is cocky
He begins to exercise more and eat differently
He indulges, but still sighs often
He is more willing to pursue a progressive lifestyle
Although he has never sustained one
And does not take his father or other employers seriously
In this twisted mind of self-worth
Sometimes cockiness yields hope
While there is honesty in sadness
There is also honesty in happiness
Gabriela thinks sometimes he likes to think
There's nothing to sigh about

Father Orange sighs, too
He lifts his arm into the sky repetitively
Bringing down with him a small piece of joy
His old life breaking his aching back
Each drupe plump and ripe
Sweeter than pure brown sugar from the East
After he'd tasted the tangiest grain and heady vapors of the sea
And known his Orange triumphed easily o'er
Boastful he was of like the matching color of the hair of his women
His wife, so lovely in spirit, always filled by his fruit
Comparable to his youngest daughter
After the three that had grown too adventurous for his farm
Gallivanting the world as he had done in youth
His son will stay working at home longer than the girls
He will loathe it and love but rue his parents
And probably leave forever, start a life of his own
But the girls might return, Father Orange suspects, in time
After the pleasures of known fulfill more so than unknown
As each orange is plump and ripe
Also he finds each a little less joyous than the last

With every respect to choice over manner,
There is always a father who never wants to hold on
And a mother who never wants to let go

Wandering

There is negativity and positivity everywhere
And in this blissful place I am lost to wonder
Why
Mosquitoes still creep up here
Not quite as dense as Southland
In most areas still to be found
And never stop biting

When hair grows long,
Wouldn't want to get it caught up

Resting together and sleeping in shifts
Pap's fur smells cleaner in this Northland air
Drifting through bushes, trees, valleys and forests
Catching his beady eye by our firelight
Wondering how much depth he sees in mine
His gaze is stupid,
Honest
He knows, although is unwilling to dwell in one stare
I usually hold attention to him longer
He focuses on me more often, and briefly
As if he's just checking
Making sure I'm still right here
Then happily becoming distracted
I can feel him near me.

And every turn
The lands of growth show a new wonder
A new mystery
This beauty holds no answers
It only seems prettier
And tastier
And possibly more tolerable

And at the same time
Gabriela finds less patience
In a hypocritical land of expansive worth

A white mint air in summer's last chapter
Flirting with the branches, rustling them
It is but for a chill
On the back of necks and upsides of wrists
That air might be so welcome here
Gabriela looks to the sky for answers,
In time to see night's black flood descend
And it was dark again

Three Oat Men

For every person who tears down a tree
So there are individuals who sow their seeds

These three characters were all from a farm
Unrelated neighbors of the common tongue
With all too-common a name, of
Oat.
And as I begin to meet them
And learn their mannerisms
Although they try to get me to enunciate
Their accents are long and strained
I cannot roll my "Os"
And I only ever called each of them Oat.

And so I name them in my head,
For whatever elusive memory
As the largest and the tallest and the widest and the wildest,
There is "bigger Oooat"
So the smaller man is "little Oat"
He is just taller than me
Pretty skinny for a farmer
And then "middle Ooat" in the middle
He is the average of the three
Albeit he has quite the riddle of a mind

Why do you watch it burn?

Gabriela says nothing as she stares into fire

You are distracted.

What?

You do not look at people.

I look at you, now.

You stare.

Oats seem like descendants of Brewers by my guess
Deduced from their manner and dislike of Pap
And adjacently he pines for attention
Until the fire warms his fur
They all nestle among bushes ascending from the ground
Or lean against a tree for succor

Middle Ooat will be easiest to first introduce
The seeds he carries grow bushes and sprout bundles of fruit
Only when the light has been shining so long
Purple and seedless are the berries that come
When grown correctly indulgences tend to come swiftly
And last half the darkness when it feels like a jiffy
The positive concept of enjoyment is misleading
Realizing one's forgotten exactly what they'd been doing

She's obsessive for intelligence
More than compulsive to it
Perhaps foolish or merely brave
So aware, too aware of something she's without
That she might try to take control
And fall to a victim of self

What do you want?

I do not know,
Nothing.

So what might you wish for?

After a pause,

I might wish I could fly, soar, like a bird
The birds don't think like we do
They just fly around catching the air
Only looking everywhere from high branches
Simply eating bugs
And being birds

And what is so wrong with that,
That you should not truly want it.

Gabriela said nothing, and then,

It's too easy.
Shouldn't we be challenged?

Ooat said nothing
To which Gabriela admitted,
Defensively,

Perhaps nothing.

And she became jealous of ignorance.

Oat Ooat and Oooat have energies of magic
I believe they are the remains of a mostly dead bloodline
They flow as if wind were wandering with us
Real as the stories of light above us
Fabulous taletellers or amazing liars
The crazy are sane and the sane are surely not
For these men merge with madness in their pondering
Not too boastful or undermining,
It would be unsympathetic to judge
Men or women of this variance
In western Southland seen as of another color
As charlatans and tramps
Bums causing overflow
Who can call blame upon sewers of seeds
To grow without plants is to sail without sea

Little Oat is short but still taller than I
He prompts more wonder, mother would disapprove
All this staring into sky

Each entity is animate
Every molecule moves
Live material in the smallest and slowest substances
But consider mosquitoes
Is biggest truly best
Is fast the finest pace
On what grounds do you judge
Your eyes are only ones you can see with

I selfishly indulge
Will I face consequence
Past the point of wickedness
Is my satisfying desire fulfilled
Of natural worldly pleasures
Are we meant to self-indulge

In this night I sip the wine of middle Ooat's fruit

I give a horribly horrific
Hopefully humorous
Disastrously detailed account
Of an unfortunate event, on my part

My mother had come over
To where Eddy and I cafuné

The Oat men, led by their eldest, snigger
She allows interruption
Gabriela rolls her glossy eyes
Tries to open them back up
Busy bodies bouncing
Behind the blinding blurry firelight

She knew of this one place we'd been frequenting
And expected to find me there,
Always when she needed something from me
Or, certainly to there I would eventually return
Our cafuné place wasn't the same place we would fuck.

Quiet, relatively respectful sniggering turns to guffaws of laughter
The unbearable mockery, she could not help herself.

A defensive tone
Troubled is a state of mind.

She pauses to find her center,
Immediately losing it
Just burbles a bit before recommencing
Trying to speak substantially over the barreling hee-haws
And continues,
With profound patience considering her audience
And the uncontrollable vomit she's drunkenly spilling

We are warm together
Mother feels the dark approaching
She finds us and sends me for blankets
Eddy wants to come but he will wait,
Mother wouldn't like us to go far away from her alone....

More laughter.

Eddy stays, I go to borrow a cart to fetch mum blankets
From this elder woman who wandered our hills
She usually left it round this bend,
Where her son was born
Hoping one day or night he'd come back for it

Now she tuned out their chortling
Gabriela knew it was for fun, esteem, and favor
She'd not let a friendly attack spoil comfortability

I pulled the cart south
With my gold, bloem, and some flints carved from rocks,
And a bushel of branches to trade with
The way was rough and I was lazy
My thoughts still with Eddy
Darkness and cold fell prematurely on my part
Well before I found someone with blankets

I illuminated the hill with a lit illinut branch
Only half-watching my footsteps
Pulled until I got caught in a rut
Tried to heave and haul but the old junk didn't budge
I could not get it unstuck from the ditch
Waiting out a third of the night there, stationary
Passersby brought blankets to me, and traded food
Until enough people could orderly dislodge it

Still intoxication made childishness laughter important
And she ended, abruptly

When I finally intend to give the cart back
I find the lady is dead
And though I doubt her son will ever return
I was inclined to leave the cart where I found it
Just in case he did

She paused for the Oats to laugh
And made room for nothing but silence
And crackling branches in the fire
They just stared at her
As if there may be more
But that was all she had to say for that stretch
Gabriela eventually passed out
Sprawled out and wasted like the lady with the cart

These objects are at your will
You can control them, should you wish
Just as you may make dirt dance
Or bend metal with your mind
This is why the mosquitoes do not bite you unless you should let them
Or why you may walk over sand instead of through it

Oooat pieced the puzzle of her expression as she ate his words

It is relative
A bird cannot control a mosquito how you may
Neither a shelio control a bird
Nor you a shelio,
No matter how much you think this animal is of your will,
It is not.

He holds his hand out
Three mosquitoes from three directions all casually bounce around in his air
To find a place to quietly land
On his palm
And there they stay unworried, undisturbed

Gabriela realized her mouth was slightly open and she closed it
Still staring,
Wide-eyed and excited

You initiated that?
This doing is of your will?

I willed it to happen,
So I let it.
...You try.

She tries too hard and fails.

Practice.

How is this possible?

And he answered this question
With a question,

What brings you to us,
To the Northland?
What has called you here
And for what logical reason do you follow?

Crisp northern-style fire
Propped up burning trees on soft forest floor
Four travelers build it, one ignites it with glass
Gabriela watches it burn
For a few hours there are only faint gestures and whispering

Little Oat eyeing Gabriela
At her look speaks loudly and calmly
Gaze suddenly shifted to the clouds,

All this energy
Around
You know, what you Know and feel

For a second he looked to the girl's pupils in the firelight again
And again spoke to the skies

It's up there, too....
That's why we can't see.

In a moment
Nothing moved but the sweat dripping down Gabriela's back
Unless it was the entirety of everything shifting around her spot
Was it true?
If she had Known it before from a dream
Seen it from above
Or heard it somewhere young....
It seemed real.
But she could not ever be sure

I got chills down me spine first time I heard it, too.

Oat's tone had changed to a taunt
Now he was kidding
How was he only pretending to be serious

The girl's face is so bemused
Three Oat men all laugh in monstrous guffaws
Glee bouncing around the circle and in the firelight

The girl believes the tale!

Calls middle Ooat.

Tales for the foolish!

Echoes bigger Oooat.

Off-put and feeling daft,
Gabriela had to ask

Is it not true, then?
What clogs the skies is not of us?

Whatever has made the clouds congregate
It is not us,

Says Bigger Oooat

Gabriela's stare is gripping the clouds
She wants to bend them, perhaps with will
But her energy is concentrated on the maximum of imagination
And she fails to prove the Oats wrong.

So strange, she thought
These men seem to Know of possibilities
Yet they think to be fooled, so they let it
Their own minds warped to conspiracy
Scared to believe anything real is true
Admitting to be in doubt themselves
I can learn much from them
Of twisted mentality
I will leave, however,
As turn these tangible clouds
Clouds they speak of, but do not accept

Bart's Road

Victor's Pass Through Dust

She has had enough grandeur
Northern esteem
As the soil turned immediately to dust
Out of the forest
Into familiar energies,
But uniquely unparalleled.

How did she know it was there?
She didn't, she thought immediately,
But she thought it was there,
And it might've been.
Or it might've been obscured.
Fat farmers
Trading from large carts
Through dusty air
She stood back
A farsighted view:
Climbing from Gap's end
'Round the forest,
And through the farms,
This was the outlet
Gabriela looked back west
The wall of earth sprung into being up from where she stood
Edgar's Gap rising from the forests and scooping upwards
It fell down a hill towards the Center and Gabriela's feet
Most appropriate place to see through dust
Amidst perfect stereotypes
In the middle of the edges
North, finer clothes
Pointed noses, rounder bellies

Haughtier air
The staircase somewhere in the distant depth of land to West
Southland
The only land slightly familiar
Yet so far through the dry valleys
It seems a half-life away
Recognizable slopes and boulders
Accents easily understood
Appropriate dealers and familiar faces
Somewhere in the depths of all that land
Gabriela's pathway, one pre-traveled
And one she destined to find worth from, for greatness
If not only for herself
From the Western Slope
The cliff curves down
As the mountain finally descends, halfway toward the sea
Southland and Northland mesh as direction narrows
In moist hills of overwhelming illinut growth
Rabid enough to not let dispute arise
Between transients and farmers
To the East, she turned finally, through the dust
To the land where sugars and spices grow north of the Illinut Hills
This must be the beginning of Bart's Road

Three thousand torches flutter 'round the Center
The middle of the solid known world, an intersection
Flaky particles luminous in the stomping ground of silhouettes,
A city
The mean and median of trades

Dangerous Road

People do not walk it together

It is not a caravan

Nor is it collaborated

Not organized or unorganized in any way

What it is,

Is a path

One way and narrow

What it materializes are: travelers; traders

Merchants, mostly

Sons and daughters

More fathers than mothers

But mostly just merchants

The men

The cart owners and their sons

And sometimes families

On road to a better, or different, place

Landlords, sometimes, strolling about
Talking with merchants
Occasionally just standing there, letting others pass
As they so strangely, like me, watch the skies
Not usually talking with Southerners
And I find mostly are pompous fools
With whom I don't care to converse

The path turns narrow, sometimes
The dirt is dry and dusty
The cliffsides are many as the way continues downhill
A steep and twisting channel
Identical means carry to inconsistent ends

With nothing to consume for stretches
But bloem from the hills or poisonous imitative plants
And sporadic morsels of seeds or a scarce choice of a fruit
The people of this pass become collective and unsupplying
Saving supplies for quantity bartering in the South and East
Here, bloem is hardly a commodity in trade
Here, people become strained with little to indulge in,
Open are their minds to tricks and pickpockets
Vulgar, dangerous ways to live by on a pathway

When baby cries
Does Mama nurture with presence or absence?
Which should baby know tomorrow?

Determination
We pick our battles
And battles of self
Everything taken its own way
Our own terms

Today, oh, what shall I do
I'm inclined to get done a tattoo
Negative demons be ridden
Kryptonite, love and might, hidden

Fortune has brought me in traveling to meet and ink many women
and men
None of which have surprised my senses
She is young but not off-putting
She is approachable,
Openly animated
Advantageously providential
I saw her twice before we engaged
It felt very late into night
She passed me for the first time on Bart's Road
And I realized with irritation by her leave
There was probably a quarter of blackness still to go
Second, for a second, around a widened bend
Meeting a merchant and trading a seed
Her hair was orange and her face white and spotted
The energy as she happened I cannot well describe
She was not happy, nor upset
She just moved along as clearly as day
Obviously present like the remaining darkness

I found my leg to be asleep as well
In the middle of my work
All these passersby
I am seeing them differently
As if I've never really known any of them before

Abandonment,
Betrayal of physical comfort
More so attaining a mental one

It gives me pain, immediately
A light, pleasurable pain that I am excited to indulge in
The process is slow, gradually shading over my back
With a permanent ink from the oils of dark seeds and the deepest buried rocks
It's my world becoming a part of me
It is a drug stuck to me
And no matter what I find on this road
I feel myself
Alone, with all of my nerves
In my own experience's experiments
I can only control myself

Sometimes even the most certain of sweets have a knack for turning sour

Although the goods I search for have eyes for elsewhere
Although bad is watching and waiting for me to succumb
There is always at least a grain of hope
Some day my pathway
May yield its fortune

Wherever those who wandered it felt they might be from and to
Whether it might lead somewhere different every time
Around another bend
Or if everything at its end was simply different over time
Whichever it was that they came or went
Coming or going, staying or leaving
Albeit a bad place to plant your feet
Here we must learn to march

They cut Pap's leg while we both slept and he could not protect me
And I refused to put up a fight
My loss of everything valuable
Bartering with rocks and bloem again
Until I can find gold to chip
Jacked in the night like a lover taken for a fool
I've still my dignity left to trade
Unless I should choose to be rid of it, too
By reclaiming my wealth at the misfortune of another
But I will never be unfair
I will always maintain my morals
At what cost will I abandon myself
Would I steal food for sustenance
If my body should need it to live, would I lie
Or should by these means
Let myself die with a clean soul
I might hope generosity of others would never let this happen
Mother taught me to trust a hope is foolishness
I do not know if I hope or not, I wonder

What They Saw Past the Hills

What we see past the hills reflects a streak of relativity
In confounding unimportance
Other past times hazy to thought
Sitting slightly blind silently squinting in light of day
As unknown slips away, brightly and sharp
All else subtle forever

No person could describe in anything other than a tone of slight insanity
It wasn't a wonder why people were unaware, no one would believe this if they heard it
Few seers truly know what their eyes behold and are ever-haunted by denial

If I fall into wonder
All else will be subtle forever
From blackness to light
Blinking day in with massive results
A warming energy shift that gives me a shudder

We have reached the edge of this path in time
Where clouds fall into the sea
To see this sky flip over
Daylight hails as everything moves around us
Flipping inside-out of darkness

A broad landscape revealed
Rounding a corner to be blasted with light
Its beauty is cracked
Chasing the horizon; futile
Gabriela has found no resolution
And upon bestowing massive magnificence
Answers fly further away

She doesn't care for the people
Their ability to destroy
Convinced in the greatness of their demising

An Account of Victoria the Benevolent

It is determined from the Family's Writings that my Siblingship is predestined to preserve the purity, Power and existence of our people. This has brought a dispute about my brothers since Vittorio was comprehensive enough to listen. What began as disagreeable spitting and pouting progressed into a wave of energy that is causing vengeance and murder in our timeful Family. No, I do not think the violence is over. For the good of the people, I suspect Vittorio has abandoned the Victor Family to start a rebellion in the South. It is Written and now assumed up to Victor: my brother Victor XIII, myself, and our sister Feli that this Thirteenth Generation do preserve for the good of the Family.

My brother Victor cannot read. He understands some of the images although the vital and complex markings; the lines, shapes and dots - He does not have patience to learn them even slightly. He has me recite, usually many times in a winter or a day, especially recently, the ancestry and chronicles of Family legend. I do not mind much, although the repetition of rules thrusting unto me a position of honor and duty grows weary. Somehow in infinite odds I am born into this, which I understand yet do not fully believe in. By carving Victor's thoughts into the Writings it has become easy to recognize my ancestors were flawed just as my brothers are. Sometimes I shudder to think of our great destiny.

Never was there a family so strong or dysfunctional as ours. As I, Victoria the Last, am meant to reform to the First, here I wait with one world to destroy and a new one to build. The thriving land and sea have filled their purposes. People have worked and built and gathered; living stupidly in conditions they do not Know. Our lies have shaped them, made what was once kinship a slaving work force, in semi-blissful ignorance for thirteen generations. What tyrannical leadership has progressed to this point has worked perfectly so far. Our decisions determine everything. But how can I watch my own people be slaughtered? And more, how can I be the one to set this cycle of madness in a congruent motion again? The future is not fated the lazy dreams of my great^{11} grandparents, though I certainly must follow through with them if I want any small slice of our civilization to continue. I cannot be rid of this inevitable gravity of purpose. My choices will rock fate. I never chose any of this.

Poor Feli, She is so young. She and Vittorio were close, although Victor was too arrogant to notice. Vittorio sympathized with Feli, among other things, and since He fled She's been unshakably frightened. I love my sister. Feli is bright, careful, and instinctive; I think Her to be the most wise of the four. Victor, around whom She is whist, would insolently disagree. Around His strength Feli may feel safe, although I believe Victor's haughty manner has turned Her allegiance elsewhere. I do not know where mine lies.

In the final days of this world I wonder of the prophesy in the Writings; if the fabled Elle will truly stumble into accompanying us.

A Giant Ship

North Beach

Fistfuls of white fluffy vapor
Scattered innocently to the west
Distance above my head, clear to gray
Up seems to stretch forever
Clouds float along the ocean, southeast
I sit between the vast sea and the world,
To the side of blind civilization
Some people nearby saying the River North is high this day
Soft waves ripple and find shape as I watch
Taking their time to roll over itself
The air here is beautiful
But there are more than enough mosquitoes for my taste

A giant ship atop the horizon
The frothy ocean of turning shlop
Dark twisted rainbows of fungus juice
Reaching forever in the daylight
Molecularly displaced energy
Boiling in the sea,
Of not really any describable color
It might be liquid, or vapor
Both cold and hot to the touch
It dissolves, or disperses
Soft, sleek, undeveloped bloem flows together

A girl alone throws herself into the sea
She emerges from juice
The high-pitched shriek that erupts from Gabriela
A sound a thousand rock bands could not drain out
Exhausted, drenched
She heaves herself aggressively into a less dramatic demeanor
A few seconds of catching her breath
Then she collapses
Pap hobbles over from a bank to lick her face
Gabriela lies on earth
Staring towards the abyss above
In nearly a complete state of helplessness
Sadness and anger built up her eyes
Instead of screaming again, she began to cower

What I think I know betrays me
It is awesome, yes
But there must be so much more to Know
An impossible amount
I cannot possibly obtain
Or prove worthy to otherwise attain

I was never really sure which direction to go
Playing off like it's all figured out
Could hardly be considered progressive
Filling time with stereotypical nonsense
Leaving me thoroughly unsatisfied
I never touched it
The horrible cliché people make of life
Will never, by me, be adopted
Determined to keep my misdirection pure
I avoid wrong
Looking for illogic in a drone's world
Finding a new concept, or
Evolving an existing one
Supposed to be conceptually worthwhile
Typical worker insects
Unsuccessful artists
Bad lives bad jobs
Wastes of effort
Living lives of lies

I crave what I cannot have
As all do
But underneath desire
Through longing
Past the shallow shores of the sea
Is an ocean of Truth
To receive my all
To gain what I want
To attain whatever I wish
Is not as fulfilling as I believe it should be
If everything I have thought I deserved
Became formed to my will
Such boons are meaningless
Splitting me farther from myself
They obscure
Blinding as I'm pulled closer
Into clutches of distraction
Pursuit of happiness
A misguided path
Away from wholesomeness of birth
Of self, and morals
Free of hope
Desire exempt
Apprehending myself
I am tainted
By love
Loss
Luxuries
So I strive to find purpose
Idea of meaning
Truth apart from the all

Pat & Pap

Watch me make this guy smack himself in the face

The mosquito spun around in midair, nodded to his comrade
Turning to face his quarry
He zoomed in a couple of clockwise spirals
Paused an instant
Then took a nose dive directly towards a forehead
Although the insect
Insanely brave for humor's sake
Was killed flat the moment he touched skin
His death was not in vain
Half a drop of his own blood on the humanoid hand
A man soon felt an itchy lump
On his facial battlefield

This shelio has been comforting
But he does not bring me joy
I must find help for him and his injury,
And be moving on

Gabriela barters passage with the bug-bitten cargoman
He pulled three carts all attached at their brackets
His shoulders were broad
And when he spoke with his booming voice
His mouth became a wide grin
Reminiscent of the quantity in his trades

A shelio would be ideal
To pull one of my carts
Protect me from robbers
And keep me company
I will fix him up

Pap took a liking to Pat
She used this moment to barter her passage
And that was that

No vice to ease this craving
Any drug just helps resent
No shoulder left to cry on
The choice is independent

Starving
Misunderstood, but not in vain
Thirsting for Knowledge
And to be from without
Liven the daily races
Grinning was ne'er enough
And now she was alone

Long Journey South

Trapped by endless darkness
Long before day was done
With the image of a new day's sky
Concealed in a ship
Light air so separate just a wall away
Unbound by clouds or worries
Unwound not by imagination
Unapproachable as a great king might be
Unbelievable as a fatal shock to the heart
The outside world thrives
Gabriela in a corner hides

A pile of fur?
No, it is a child
Quite small,
Conclusively deceased
A chameleon of the ship's gray and brown floor
Alone, thoroughly helpless
Ransacked, trampled, faceless, possibly semi-melted
Fully incapable of the faintest squeak
Is her presence here searched for? Missed? Known?
She is watched over by a nearby doorframe, an entryway to the next room
And here she will rest
Until chance or significance comes to sweep her away

I do not fear death, I fear pain
The excruciating euphoria throughout life
Pains, both physical and mental, are inevitable
As careful as I can be
I cannot control what happens
I know only to be conscious of fate
I realize that I Know nothing
I understand how but do not have means of protecting myself
Everything is understandable
Nothing is Knowable
Am I awake? Am I dreaming?
On one level, not all of them.

Every several moments the ship pulls ashore
To unload several dozen travelers
I think the girl watching from the corner
Is waiting for the last stop

To weep myself to sleep
To doze a dozen slumbers
Cursing Truth does no better than hiding from it
Craving to cry until dry skin cracks
To scream until my insides twist
But mostly I just want to stop hurting
Part of me cares not for my woes in the world
For at times I feel unnecessarily fine
Brushing off things that make me unhappy
Cheerful in spite of it all
And then dragged back
Like a rag doll leaving herself to fate
Just hoping one day the waiting will prove to be over
And there will be something real to live for

Sometimes
Probably most of the time
Thirst is for Truth
Hunger for Knowledge

East Southland

Excessive Mercantilism

There is bustling, hustling
And everywhere
On an overcrowded path
A swift sliver of ground seen for a second
And then madness
People and what they carry
Pile off the ship and pile on the ship
And Gabriela in the flow
Barely stepping with her own feet
Stench of muggy stirred and disturbing
She finds her arm and plugs her nose
And holds her pocket so as to claim
Whatever a sticky finger may try to remove

Any trustful air of Gabriela seceded.

Mostly Mercantile
They all seemed to know where they were going
Or at least
A general direction of it

Gabriela tried turning to look back at the ship
But it was lost behind the tall heads of ten thousand traveling

For an endless moment the pathway was narrow
Northward moving, the merchants from the beach
All together along the Long River North

Janus

Her feet soon found earth as the density dispersed like a delta
Scattering bodies in search of a fresh air
And for the second time in her life,
Gabriela learned to march.
To march is to walk with a destination or purpose
Gabriela's march was a dance of escape
As she marched for nothing more than to be allowed to stop
But not near this shift surely
Stoppage would mean to be trampled

Come with me.

He grasps her firmly but with grace
She knows not to trust yet lets go
And follows with the strong energy that intrigues her now
Through all the ruckus and out of it

He leads her, holding her firmly, and with grace
Pulling her slowly, so she may gather him
Escorting her to his home,
East of river, she lets him bring her, now
To never let her go, firmly and with grace
And no longer let suffer their desires

This man who has taken me
Ahold of my hands up a road farther east
His touch I permit
And our bodies follow each other
Through this instant passionate energy

I can see from the other side
Over the waters
Illuminated on the dock there
Three standing figures
I recognize the largest one
The other two are strangers
A young girl, radiant, graceful, looking onto the tide
Fires shining from miles away let it sparkle slightly even in day
Another figure looks this way and that
To her, the water, or o'er his shoulder, to the bonfire
And up and down, arbitrating the tree
His hands are deep in his pockets

Jewels in Gabriela's eyes as she gazes into waters
Bubbles emerging around each other,
Dangerously falling back down beneath its busy surface-
To nearly immediately ripple over-top again
Gabriela moves on the bank for a closer look
Checking behind to make sure Janus won't push her in
He is looking at her; she cannot tell his expression
She feasts back on the eyesoring juices

Janus feels lint in his pocket
He fiddles with it momentarily
Disregarding it, decides instead to bite his lip
He looks up and down the dock, which does no good
He lets his lip go and puts a foot forward
Not meaning to go anywhere
Trying to react, he stumbles a bit
And Gabriela looks back at him again
Luckily he's recovered in time to a full standing position
So he looks into her face with nonchalant meaningless
An empty look he sometimes gave her
Damn those eyes.
Janus looks down on them with all his might
They are blazing into his with the hottest of fires
It is difficult to prevent himself from faltering again

A little discouraged at blankness
Though far from put out
Gabriela turns away once more
To watch the beauty of the Long River North

The tree stands out of the water
Easily recognizable
Tall and strong, displaying its shape over the dock
Bold and irrelevant over two respectfully young figures
It did not care about the people it fed, nor sheltered
It did not think much at all
It just stood
Tall, strong, content

I think about Gabriela
I try to think about Linda
Brianna
Analise
And Tracy
And I can't stop thinking about Gabriela
And all of the things I love about her
Imagining alternatives and trying to focus on her flaws,
It isn't working

He watches her figure in the light of day at the brim of the reflecting pool, obsessing
Air gently lifted her hair in the most precious of ways
Part of him wants to call to her
But he must deny the falsehood of every feeling she fills him with

Gabriela breathes deeply
Trying to remain calm in the quiet day
She's no inking to the direction of his thoughts

We might fish,

Says the man

And they did it beneath the tree

Why do I continue to say yes? A fool's hope, deep down
You push me until I'm ready to break and fall away
The turning point comes, and your arms are pulling me back

As clearly as our desires are pleased,
Honesty is visible.
We cannot keep each other
Knowledgeable of my means of subtle satisfaction
Peace of mind if not of soul
I cannot stay with you
In this sense
My choice has elsewhere been abandoned
Letting go here would be insulting
As if leaving something good for something better
I promise nothing to these lands, or any
But lack of my attachment
I cannot be lost or left behind
Everything hangs around, hovering over
My hazed memory dangles the sharp Truth
Whatever
If I cannot curl my own hair
If I cannot blow my own mind
If I must be one with another other than me
There is a man in the western Southland
Who has already succeeded in this

Merely one she already has
And does not need but wants
She does no not want to need and also
In sense she needs to want
Desiring nothing more
Than the nothing that already is
She still wants to have everything
And everything to give

How can this be ending
When it's barely even begun
In fact it hasn't even started
Yet it's ending, over, done
I'm hung up on your kiss
Your gentle grips
The way you bite my lip
There was hope in your love
That I want to take for myself
And it's faded?
As hope does
It's over,
Overrated.

Where do I expect to meet
Someone to sweep me off my feet
The ones I've met before today
I've managed to scare them all away
If oh, just once, there was a girl
Who'd twist my whiskers so they might curl
I'd show and teach a thing or two
Of all the real things I can do
I'd make love to you in the heat
I'd fuck you naked in the street
T'would be considered rather rude
If I neglect to find your food
We'll get you fed and get you high
Goosebumps quiver when I stroke your thigh
We can meditate, contemplate, conjugate, and argue
Believe, agree, and disagree without a clue
Articulate definition
Breakthrough ambitions
Refuse to live anew
Play with life
Uncaring what's untrue
Lustful strife
Before we e'er unglue
Before either of us withdrew
Our brains we'd wrap askew
We'd talk of a new tattoo
Whether luck might come from shelio
Where the best illinuts grew
No curfew
We'd fly there
From midair
Nothing obscured
Each other endured
Through passing days we'll mature
And out of the air
To do what we will as we dare
But my hair does not curl
I fear fate leaves it straight
If good things come to those who wait
I guess we'll see when we get there

This is not a game to me
And there's someone else who curls my hair

Facing around, but then
She turns back

You cannot wait for Good
Either it happens, and let it
Or you must seek it yourself

Sticky Fingers

Rule makers, only ones who got there first
Guidelines are unimportant
When you are separated from society

Janus is restraining
Forbidding me to leave
Try as I might to stifle his rage
The insanity in his face is of anger, madness

He claims,

We torture ourselves
Idealize and believe hopes and myths
Let ourselves down
Or lie, and let ourselves down harder later
We are trying to grasp, rest on concepts
We are trying to store faith in nouns and pronouns
And we sprint
Soon to find the direction we think correct, irrelevant
And it is better for us to stand, still, and be
Just be here
Our present, now
Expanding: the only productive thing to pursue
Nourishing our failing bodies to ensure a greater span of time
We study and listen to gain the wisdom to be still
Pray for nothing and believe in everything
As we know a lighter Good in our lives might arrive
After we've punished ourselves enough in this place

I did not mean to inspire such Evil out of you
You mean to twist happiness out of desperation
My captivity will give you no satisfaction

His retaining sustains

My heart may be sane
But your head is not with it
So I'll turn metal down your throat
Fearing my hands aren't ready
But they must be anyway
This has got to be done
I've been steering my ship
And now you control it
Aggression drove us to this
If it was not me, or you, it would be the next
Will to kill is the will to be spared
I always had to do this
I had to feel your cold, sweaty, real hand in mine
To be sure I may escape
I needed to see the light leave your eyes
To be present for your last curse
To hear your final breath
You are wasted and dead and bloody in my lap
Running a dozen brown strands through my fingers
I curl one time over and release
The anger from your face has vanished
As I feared it never would
You appear clear, and peaceful
This is what you wanted, which I envy
Deep down you felt you had to be stopped
Yet if I was ever given the choice
My heart could not have broken yours
As you will not break mine
It was sense, not love, which triggered me
I let you go and flee
Enough mourning has been done on your part in life
My thoughts will never again include you

Memory,
So elusive,
Do not let collapse
The castle of cards
We built these delusions on
Ones that comforted us
Dreams of who we thought we were Lessons
served to us by a knife
Stabbing us with glints of our own reflection
Let never fade who I become
As my tower stacks taller
Kings and Queens find their places
Every narrow edge balances delicately Will
compulsively crumble at once
Fallen to a heap
What was once our space and time
And from it I will build
A new castle

Home

Shiloh the Shelio

Wandering tranquilly alone around the road
Smiling snout panting heavily
Exhausted by his own excitement
Bored of freedom and loneliness

As if to meet only to dismiss
She could not replace Pap
Nor was this the time to acquire responsibility

Gabriela crosses people's pathways to approach the shelio
Who allows her cosset for a moment
While he licks at her hair
His tongue is slimy with bumps
His fur, sleek brown with spots

This pause is intimate and fleeting
As after this occasion
Both parties flee to unrelated futures

Stretch

Knowing there may be a fizzling disappointment of an end
But expecting an ending nonetheless

What remained
Long shot potential of true connections
For him to be near would be unreal
Although a longing emotion of reason
Drove her on, and on
Her tongue was dry
Thoughts racing and repeating
If she was honest with herself,
Accounting actions as irrationally disturbing
She's approaching nothing, anywhere
But perhaps a fizzling disappointment

Having to go back to move forward
Onward is a mysterious direction
But there, home will have changed
Similar, but not alike
A secret plot of earth
I knew a place like this, once
Mold grows similarly
Shrubbery just as crackly
This area I stumbled upon is new to me
The only direction I know is the long one I've come from
I must be moving on

As the day feels endless
Eventually the rough land becomes recognizable
Air breathes easily
Memory shifts to light
As familiar turns to known
Remembering slopes of the grounds
Metal gardeners and workers I hardly care to stop for
Passing a handful of half-recalled people
Finally I slowed my pace,
Feeling, here, some realm of a changed home

This area seems less crowded than before
After the long stretch
Body and mind weak, but cleansed
This place radiates comfortable energy
Blasting me with compassion
Filling me with hope
And equally,
Hopelessness.

Searching for one person in half a million
Would I check the usual spots and squats
How long would I endure looking
before searching for something else
And what is to befall us
Should we meet
Only to search for a way to pass the time

Gabriela abstains from locals
Strangers or not
She destines not to mingle
Listening naught but for that distinctive voice
One she does not need but wants
Looking for nothing but Eddy's curls

And when she knew not what was to be there

Close, approaching like a magnet

He was

Dream Smoke

Edward's face had grown long

Two long days
And two endless stretches of dark depressing night
We have been gone from here,
Gone from each other
Strange new places, faces, routes, foods, moods,
Circumstances agonizing alone, away
Just looking at you inspires me

His face curled into a smile
Skin stretched aged worried wrinkles
New grin of relief
Lifting cheeks causing him to squint
Finally reunited

See into my eyes
As they are loving and honest
Believe their twinkle,
As need be, I plea
Your eyes have been so fixed to the back of my head
Still so unsure
Turns I haven't turned yet
I won't turn
Loving and honest, forever I'll be
Give me this chance
Let me be with you
Again, and again
Over and over
Night in and day out
Charmed to live and be a fool for you

Demise is everywhere, fool
All are conceivably selfish to cruelty
If you doubt your wrathful potential
Evil will enthrall you
Your lust will suffocate me
Or we will kill each other with kindness
Promises forever ask to be broken
Our beauty flourishes only in split seconds
Beauty is cursed

If split seconds are all we have
I'll waste mine with you
Until you shoo me away
And I'll let you go again, respectfully
Let you be where you'd rather
Maybe never to meet again....

I'd rather nothing
Here, now, works
Fleeting moments
Would be nice to continue forever
Would be nice to never say goodbye
Never miss
Only be in endless bliss
The communication we feel through a kiss
Only each other together forever
Trapped in a thought loop of harmlessness
Responsibility and consequence dissolved
How could any of the whole be at all essential
If worries and hopes should be so erasable
I just want to love
Be together in mind, body, and what I can only hope is an everlasting soul
Chase the clouds, up and away
Run from nothing, for nothing
No gain or loss, only presence
Only the moment
The space and time we occupy today
The thing we feel, we know we must appreciate
This fleeting life
I don't want to spend it, whither it, waste it away worrying, or in vain
I just want to love

I search for meaning
And let it evade my life
Half-distracted
Convinced it absent to begin with
Now I wish to have purpose here
Releasing my thoughts of overcoming love
Truly I must be alone, certainly
As I feel isolated in my core
However I long for connection
And my thoughts are ever-twisted like this
In loops of confusion
I wish I can thoroughly be content
With my own intention
Be not victimized, questioning, unconfident
Allowing you to bring me happiness
This shouldn't be too hard
If I'm doing it right there'll be no effort in it.

Love is strong in weakness,
That we should leave trust in the company of another
If you'd rather nothing
Let us smoke the dream plant
Indulge entirely, being
Together forever
Amidst honest Knowledge
Let true happiness come
And, Knowledge.
For without tragedy, there is no comedy,
Without heartbreak there is no love,
And without longing there is no desire
We can find everything in nothingness

This is nearly effortless,

He said,

And then it will be.

Her unquestioned answer
Yes.
Letting go
Gabriela was without fear of the unknown
Dream plant, purple and green and blue
Had since looked so foreign
In her possession now at ease

Break, clouds!
So I can see the light, the expanse
The universe
I want a perspective of our galaxy
I do not want to hide here
I want to leave, and
Never come back

Greeting as a long lost friend she'd never met
Gabriela helped Edward arrange branches
Handling her indulgence carefully while glass ignites the fire

She holds it to the flame
Allowing the sparks to bounce into her cupped hands
Purple and green leaves disintegrating immediately to smoke and ash
Gabriela breathes it in

Her mind raced
A feeling to revere
She tried to remain fixated on her space
Could not sustain concentration of the place
Reality began to interfere

It came to her as an entity
She recognized it
But did not remember it

The things I am thinking of
I am remembering
Are they my memories?
Am I imagining them?
Do they belong to anyone else?

Are we circling or spiraling
When we see yellow
Yellow is all we determine
Yet is the only thing
That isn't there to be seen
We know what we see
We Know it's untrue
Yellow was always absent
Never the front
Everything else is
With the naked eye, study abyss
Passersby and land and sky
We Know of more
But are unsure to think
Fearful of greatness
Put in our place by physical size
Restricted by dimensional minds
Hoaxed by our own kin
We know nothing of Knowledge

The line
The technicality
Dividing a gray area
Stands for nothing
Parts nothing
Objectifies nothing,
But itself.

When all you can see is right in front of you
Your life dedicated
Your soul attached
Your happiness dependent
Will it be your comfort in this world
Or your discomfort
What is left to dwell on but your own well-being
And mysteries of fate

Do we truly want to sense

Do we truly want to Know

Do we truly want to be

Have wisdom and Knowledge

Lust for food, sex, or drugs

Need for any presence of body

Have I been trapped within, praying to be without?
Or does to be without come with a longing for presence?
Surely to be without is to be without consciousness...?

What do you do with all the information you see
Do you retain it
Your soul is so beautiful but your mind is broken
Embrace,
Do not despise,
Imperfection.

Zen in circles of unknown comforts
Alien familiarities ease the sense of eeriness
Dancing without feeling ground
Flying without sky
Deep in unfamiliar adventure
Alone with everything and deeper
A plunge of forfeiting will
Powerless to the beauty of soul
And ever-expandable mind

In long life things tend to repeat
Conversation grows repetitive
And the imperfections of a stranger are reminders of an old friend

Finite patterns, curves and shapes
And in these circles there is opportunity to learn
What you could not have seen before

Wandering blind,
All of these leaders keep following people
Left to time's fate, at her convenience

This is not the last time I will make these mistakes
They are part of me
And will repeat respectfully
My trust, or my mistrust,
My emotions gathered to burst
I am only one person
A creature of the fungal sea
Evolving with the world around me
And the natural mannerisms that shape my path

Knowing all of these things outside
What's to be seen in life
All of the work and things to be done
With the strong-heartedness of a wife
Thinking of a new mystery
Something unsolved and misunderstood
Using big words and deep feelings
Unsure if we should
Listening to the weather
Beauty, or lack there of
Falling with angst and hatred
Or fighting with sincere love
Putting every emotion into words
Letting thoughts out of their cage
With expression, meaning, sympathy
Pinnacles of your age
And even when every significant notion
Is recorded in a permanent ink
Sit, relax, recount your words
For they're not as conclusive as you think
Maybe your life is a mystery
Or an exciting underdog tale
Travels, controversy, all of it's there
So it's hard to admit you have failed
All your feelings, all your thoughts
Have all been thought before
One may think on end for a day or two
And never think of more
We're all living in one world
And to us it is the same
Whatever rules we make of it
We're still playing a game
We're all born and we live
We all think, eat, pray, and feel
That is all and this is it
Everything we can Know to be real
Nothing new will come to light
For what can be seen, we see
One may live in the clear or hidden by shadow
But all we can do is be.

I dreamed I'd never found you
I dreamed I was alone
I dreamed of a labyrinth without you
Doomed to navigate home on my own
I'm sleeping, eternally dreaming
Pretending I know nothing about
The reality where I can be with you
For now, my dreams leave me without
I suffer in this dark place of Truth
Unreality, impossible to take up
The longer I continue this dreaming
I'm finding it hard to wake up
The more I'm forced here to see
The less of it I seem to feel
Roots sprouted from my feet, and shading branches of my arms
Hidden from what I know to be real
I cannot fall out of substance
Searching life for one true thing to tell
I cannot forget place away from this time and space
I will wake and reunite with Elle

An Account of Vittorio the Vital

My brother is obsessed. He cannot by my means come to realize the ignorant arrogance of our ancestors. What Victor XIII does not understand is, although by seizing Power ambitions may be attained, Power is not everything.

Not many can turn flames at their touch, nor for nutrition ingest them. I burn a feather. Birds were surely such strange, stupid creatures. Flames escape, black and blue flames, with orange. Mouthing a prayer, I capture in my grasp a favorable one, let it trickle down my fingers, down my palm, and I taste and swallow it. Light, warm; comforting; it never quite hits the spot.

Victor would have never thought to utter devotion. To pay respects to something intended to produce His allowances is apparently entirely unnecessary. The only thing He ever considered important is His, our, direct bloodline. It is the culpability of our notoriously illustrious parents to be thanked for the manufactured belief of destiny. I appropriately slit their throats in their sleep.

I taught Feli how to read The Writings, the history of our Family. As soon as I understood what it meant to our Siblingship, I taught it to Her. She picked it up much more quickly. While I honestly tried to remain unbiased, she is wholeheartedly devoted to my cause, my hope for us, that we can bring enough energy together to sacrifice ourselves for the good of what will inevitably be destroyed.

Victoria knows of Feli's allegiance but not of my plan. Confused with indecision, hopefully promptly, She will choose what idea to betray. Eventually She'll come to understand, and remember what has clouded even Her memory. I rely on Feli to work with Her and continue an uprising. The arrangement in works will rock fate; Victoria will soon see how.

ARISE, ALL IN THE SOUTH! AND BE WITH YOUR KIN. GOODNESS SLEEPS AMONG YOU. PEOPLE IN SOUTHLAND WILL RISE TO DEFEND THEIR HONOR AND PURPOSE. THOSE IN THE NORTH WILL BE FOOLED INTO DECEPTION BY WHOM THEY FOLLOW. KNOW YOUR OWN TRUTH. DESTRUCTION IS NEAR, REGARDLESS. FIGHT FOR YOUR FREEDOM! MARCH TO THE CENTER OF THE WESTERN SLOPE. FEAR NO ONE, AND NOTHING, AND NOT DEATH, FOR SURELY TO BEFALL EVERYONE IS DEATH. FIND YOURS WITH VALIANCY. AWAKE FOR INTEGRITY! AWAKE FOR THE SOUTH!

Reawakening

Flat Infinity

She cares not of surrounding consequence
Energy humanoids create accidentally or consciously
For Elle, other actions are irrelevant

The world is alive around her
She is consumed by her own bubble of exhaustion
Her eyes, already squinting from firelight, droop
Her deepest desire was to let them close....

My ears are burning
I want no destined glory
I want no great treasure
I want to consume nothing
All self-desire stripped
For morsel, cushion, or pipe of air,
Am willing to strive gravely to be without
My womanliness has been diminished
My wrath is crushed and forfeit
I'm lying flat to the planet
Despair around causes me pain
There is nothing for it
I get up and run
Any might, any strength I possess
Stretched in muscles of aching body
Imagination has been erased
My mind is shut off
Nearly entirely
But for a prick in back of my eye
Embodying my outer awareness
Grueling embodiment
Ogling and staring
My feet are bare
Space-worn clothing and colored sweaty face
Drawing attention
I am bothering people
If it is not the tattered state of my attire
The sharp momentum of my sprint
The general trampled look of my body
My expression of intensity is scaring passing company
I am in shock again, or still
As Truth is imprinted inside of me
The limited being I possess aches
I cannot be calm or collected
I am frantic
I crave privacy

Running though the area
Ignoring the failing trades
Power gaining intoxications
Fatally doomed workers
The merchants
The travelers
The artists
Young, and old
And stupid
And unsure
And in the back of my thoughts
Like a waking dream
My mind becomes
For a moment
Clear
And I see it
A hill too steep to infest
Too high and dry to harvest
Thousand fires viewpoint
A serene place
As isolated as anybody could find
One solitary wild stem grows
Alive, alone
Colorful against the dead hillside
Unreality is a fleeting fraction of time
Beginning to wonder
Was it only a state of mind
Striding up and around to the top of a rocky knoll
It is surely that hill in the distance
Away from the bustling
Tightly packed lifestyles
A good spot to just be
Perhaps to gather myself.

I am not alone here,
I was followed

Her air is familiar and feels safe

I do not Know nor care how
For no more Evil or Good could possibly come to me in this life

To be forgotten
The stories of my parents
My own mind is lost in a haze of time
White and blackness have erased memory of my dreams
Everything else is left
Knowledge remains,
Lost somewhere in the confines of my frail body
Truth glints obviously in my eyes
Making them burn and water
Finally able to tear

The elusive memories of my past
Feel as if they're from another life
Not on this plane
This lover that chases behind me
I have never felt less close to
Where is my mind?

I used to feel things
The feeling remains only relatively
Now I feel myself in relation to everything else,
Everyone else
Nothing is unimportant
But essentially all is insignificant
Happiness, it's a riddle
Desire is a joke
If we wanted what we had there'd be no need for more
A man's quest for gain self-equates
We trick ourselves into self-satisfaction
There is nothing for us
Only what we create
And I always found disappointment more often,
Questioning
We all might as well sit down.

She spoke slowly,

I am grateful now
To claim neither possessions
Nor desire of glory
Everyone over-thinks
Their needs escalate
Trying to be blissful?
Knowledge concentrated on furthering this goal,
Madness!
All is a quest for happiness
Plagued beneath and between the airs of deceit
All of them are trying to get somewhere,
Somewhere they are already being stopped from getting to.

Just
Enough trial and error
Emotional rebellion
Troublesome woes
Enough good company
Gray sky of emissions
Air supply, and nutrition
Just!
Enough of everything
In the dreamed world
To relax apart from
Enough nothingness
Alive in slumber
To be centered in oneself
Enough consciousness
Here, now, ever
To just exist with

How Edward's Hand Felt

Did you wake me?

Yes, but I don't know how I Knew to.

Knew to what?

Call you Elle.

I will never be famed, rich, or successful
Luck may never find me and stay
The pathway will remain unclear
Never to be sure where I'm going
Inevitably misinterpreting my past
According to my own understanding
Everything will change
Everything will falter from plan
Everything will be alright

The loss of the feeling of utter well-being
Entranced by the past
Nothingness could not last
With ups come the downs
With downs come regret
After life in the light
Now the darkness has set
A cancerous tumor of love was the rumor
Now tripled in size
Like the pupils in your eyes
The expression of joy
That of which you did taste
Has swallowed the natural
I'll not let this life amount to waste

The stem emerges two inches above the world
Nowhere near any area that should allow it
Elle considers with a fingertip
Wild life growing in a desolate place
Where bloem are scarce, the only plant around
Surviving from underground
Reason of how is unattainable
Reason of Good and Evil, immaterial
Her eyes penetrated Edward
She plucked the stem without flinching
And he watched her toy with it pointlessly
Finally tearing it into itty-bitty pieces

It was my fault
I'm sorry
I need to make it up to you, Elle

Fault is a pointless persecution
As praise is equally insignificant
To pass blame on accidental, purposeful, or instinctual actions
Or praise them
Everyone should already be exempt for performance
From judgment
Reward
Condemnation
Spite
Forgiveness
Or prejudice.

That's my name.

Elle.

He said it appropriately.

Elle,

He sang, and looked at her.

She looked at him.
And when he took her hand, her fingers and her palm, in his
A familiar feeling she Knew though did not remember
It was lovely, intimate, sexy
Gently, honestly adoring
It was rough and more burned than two days ago
But still, it was Edward
It, was.
Real.
She found a small comfort to his touch
Slightly less suffocated by herself
Somewhere deep in his eyes she saw reason
And he saw the same in her

I just had an inkling to say it.

The information of Edward's Knowledge
Danced like a flame,
Flickering thoughts to his mind.
Elle was right.
Wherever she said they needed to go,
He would follow her and he would help her.
There was nothing to stop him this time
For Truth was here
Some form of something he already Knew
Was here
He was in the works
He felt meaning, purpose
He was here for her,

And so Elle Knew there was purpose in her Power.

Another Departure

What madness is this?

The baritone torches
Alive in the night
Dangerously close to the crop

Men pace around us
Wearing travel-tattered cloaks
And expressions of muddled anger and purpose

What calls you to disturb my family
On my land
As we are resting?!

The men do not change their expressions
There are at least a dozen of them
They seem eager to catch my stalks on fire

Have your wife and each child harvest and gather all they can carry,
Prepare for life anew; bring provisions, seeds, bloem,
Leave behind weighty personal possessions,
There are no exceptions.

Are you robbers?

We are here for your protection.

And what of my daughters?

There can't be any exceptions.
They must carry all they can.
Also, bring your axe

Unsettled by the moment's strangeness, by way of fear
Instructions to my family are to obey the transients
To follow with them, leaving us placeless
We are all frightened
The men, and smoke from the east, encourage us to move quickly
The few moments proceeding are a haze of the burning lands of my ancestors
And the muddled fellowship of neighbors
We walk away together, wandering toward war
Wide-eyed, whispering, whimpering, wondering
Completely unsure, trading rumors
And watching our world burn

AWAKE, PEOPLE OF NORTHLAND! AND BE WITH YOUR KIN. HARVEST AND GATHER ALL YOU CAN CARRY. TRUST NO ONE AND NOTHING. DESTRUCTION IS NEAR, REGARDLESS. ALL WILL FALL TO THE CENTER OF THE WESTERN SLOPE. ABANDON THE OLD TO PREPARE FOR LIFE ANEW, A FRESH GROWTH; BRING PROVISIONS, SEEDS, BLOEM. FORTIFY YOUR ARMS SHOULD YOU NEED TO DEFEND YOURSELF AGAINST VENGEFUL SOUTHERNERS. DESTRUCTION IS NEAR, REGARDLESS. YOUR SIGNIFICANCE IN THE WORLD IS INEQUAL TO THE VICTOR FAMILY.

They burned the fields
The history
They would not fall victim to Southern Rebellion
One way or another
Everything would have to start over

It was not in Victor's message
Although all the same to Him
The Northerners burn their crops as they evacuate
He did not see the irony behind their objective;
Bravery, love, remembrance, personal principle
He could not see their purpose

Traveler Shifts

Semi-Familiar Route

Fuzzy memories of roads in western Southland
Unrecognizable by the odd traffic moving northeast
They do not follow the crowd
Gabriela leads Edward through a thinned-out land
Avoiding looking for trouble
If destiny must be, it would find her
As she is drawn to it now
Knowing she is Unknowing

A man pulled a cart a few areas away
His load emptied,
Perhaps they might barter an easier journey
Armed with as many provisions as fit in Edward's bag
As Gabriela carried the gold
They had been running northwest
Restless; overdue

Might we trade for a ride

Unlikely
What are you called
Where are you from

She motioned cautiously
Alternative to presumptions
This merchant, these people...
Something was wrong

We are from this western land, south of here

Gabriela dug into his eyes with her own for an answer
But received no clue
He hid nothing
He showed nothing
Why did he not care to ask what they trade?

I don't take anything!
It's no worth, in the North
Nobody's buying anymore

The man was barking
T'was not the weight of the cart so bothersome
And perhaps not the frightening superstition of night
There was a deeper worry

Sir, I assure you...

She spoke as calmly as possible
Which must have thrown him off
Her docile, young tones

I don't carry seeds or weeds
Nor bronze or steel
My gold is of fine quality

Gold?

All at once his ears perked up
A bit of his face drained in color
Illuminated by firelight from nearby

Yes, sir

He had been underestimating
Betwixt trust and foreboding
She never altered her gaze

You might have some luck with that
Who knows, now
I hear, they say
Gold may still be flowing

He paused,
Unsure, apparently
Should he have let his guard down so much
Even against a young woman

But sorry, ma'am
I'm not giving any rides today
Not for metal, no
Can't trust circulation
Best of luck to you

Over the rocks he pulled his cart
And away,
Quickly,
He went

On a bit further
What was that whisper?
How frustrating
To never be able to rewind time
Sometimes men speak so quickly
I'd like to hear them twice, these secrets!
How obnoxious
To be unable to slow time down
As the fleeting moments are let to elapse
Time, she is unbendable
With this will

Sweaty, sore, worn
Stretch a bit but can't hide the smell
I am tired, physically
But contrary to miserable
In lieu of boredom
I chuckle
At the passerby weakly staring at the ground
Not encouraged by it continuously holding up

There then came a great quake.
Progression stopped
Insanity did not ensue
As one
As one has bravo and cun
Bent to the ground
On one knee or two
Or sprawled on their backs
Cradling their necks
Curled up into a ball
With what should positively have been fear
The people rocked dangerously
Swaying in place
But did not run and twist their ankles
In an eternal instant
Elle and Eddy understood
This must be the second quake

From long ago there are fables of an attack
Who's to say it would not happen again
Forgotten
Epic battle
Escape only on a whim
The martians are back
Ready for complete annihilation
We will not be preserved by a hymn

What madness is this
It is spreading
Air thick with the energy of panic everywhere
And silence
People are wide-eyed as if hopeful for help
But unable to trust any
What madness is this

She watched the Käufer house burn.
She witnessed as mad men threw torches through windows;
Dancing and singing hallelujah to the god of mayhem
With her own eyes she'd seen a roof engulfed in orange and blue air
And black and blackest smoke,
Stoked by the hateful something
Of the worst kind of people.
There it was;
That something,
That distinction between Yes and No
The one that boiled blood,
Too hot to handle.
That same something driving on
That changed the air from place to place
And from person to person, day to day;
It was dancing out of the windows
It was creeping around the corners
Distastefully licking the walls and breaking through the banisters
You build a home, it collapses in on you
Something crumbled a legacy

Climb

Again she reached the secret staircase
Far west and massively tall on the slope

Together two beings stared upon a vast wall
Large as any on their land

Oh, aching body
Why do you contort me so
Why must you keep heaving heavy breaths
And fluttering shutters of my eyes
Constantly unable to believe everything at once
Why is my mind closed to proximity
How may I see through
Time, area, realm
Can I exist there,
Without this body
Not now, it seems
But perhaps I can exist here, with
Driving on instinct
Following my path
Albeit leading aimlessly
Failure has been inconceivable
Shepherding my shadow
Up steps recognized
As if from another life
But not my own

She seized her awkward body and pulled herself up

My body will ache and crumble

Until my mind has also been exhausted

My physical being an irrelevant piece of matter

No longer possessing the strength to contain me

My soul will escape, with free reign, if I should let it

Into an abyss I had to accept I do not Know

An existence exponential to my dimensionally restricted delusions

Illusions, of reality

Assembly

All at once
Again atop the natural staircase
Clarity ensues in a perplexing way
She was of course meant to be here
There was no longer any doubt
Whether she chose this destiny or it chose her,
Here it was
And what was to happen
Elle must unquestionably act somehow
As she always Knew she should,
This reality was evidence
As bewildering as the sight affront

The forest burns
It has mostly disappeared
Eastward I can see a full path of people
Climbing west over otherwise desolate hills
Along a fire-lit path
Through what surely is
Salvaged farms
Abandoned lands
What were once flourishing homes of families
There is an energy of sorrow,
And a trace of fear in every step

We've been in this hell long enough
We've all driven ourselves crazy
Mesmerized
Sacrifice
Something must be wrong
Worry in the air has multiplied
We are unsure what rescue or torment is to befall us
But something, surely, soon
Or we'll suffocate on our own confusion

It's lottery now
Look, skill, experience, intelligence;
They will not be escorted anywhere
There are so much of all these things,
Respectfully,
Too much to the point
Where all of it means nothing
It's up to chance, and luck
For rescue, or damnation

We circle each other until one attacks
I dreamed this

ALIVE, EVERYONE! AND BE WITH YOUR KIN. ALL OF YOU HAVE BEEN DECIEVED. GOODNESS SLEEPS AMONG YOU. BE AT PEACE WITH YOUR OWN TRUTH AND WHAT YOU DO NOT KNOW. DESTRUCTION IS NEAR, REGARDLESS.

At the Center
In a secret underground place there was a massive metal box
Circular, huge, hidden for the boss
The earthquakes had caused the cavern to quake
And now a sinkhole dismantled the land
Cavity to the underground
Cavern, caved in
The great metal dome remained
Dark, mysterious and quite suspicious
There was no nearby sea for this ship to roam
Really nowhere feasible for it to go

The Western Slope is destroyed and overrun
With flames and bodies
Madness and mayhem
Chaos and karma
Fear is on fire
And so is the land
Broken, divided
Desperate gestures
And panicking tempers
Badly hidden or fighting
Mistrust is everywhere
Asking questions to dismiss their answers
No impulse seems rational
People already starting to decay

And some are already courageous and brave

Direction seemed lost in many a' minds
Afore the platform atop the ship
"Yes, of course" were their pleas
As any one insisted they need to pass

Once what has been decided
And why is unimportant
How is just a matter of having the will to do.

Escape

Black Gold

Have you thought
This wholly seems unwise
Trying to help people
Who would leave us for dead

We've made it this far
Perhaps there is hope

What do you expect to do by sleuthing into a ship?

We know that we can't Know
Of a greater presence in the universe
Than what we already aware of
So all that is left
Whether or not
To give ourselves up
Believe
End any personal quest for happiness
Overcome self-importance
Be humble beings
Know our place
Our purpose
May be for another, others, and everything
We are not meant to live only for our own sakes
We can make it right, balanced
On a whim of instinct

I will follow your impulse
To whatever end
Right or wrong, we're goners here....

Do not shy away from presence
If you must be rid of it, rip it away
Respecting your adversary

On a pathway to death
Everything seems familiar
And repetitive
And more consequential

And by basic energy of will
Knowledge of what she'd always Known
She used this Power to come to this, the Center

At the gates of madness
Gabriela meets the men guarding it
Direct Victor minions
Submissive to this Balance of Power

None shall pass

I must pass.

NONE shall pass

Relatively, play to your opponent

What are they paying you, to die standing here?

They raise their weapons

...I mean only to pass, and no harm
You may take my gold, it is all that I carry
Its value will be nothing when this night is over
I promise that Truth is more than the Victors offer.

They raise their eyebrows, but do not lower their weapons

None. Shall. *PASS.*

And in the middle of the mania
With no mental effort
She holds her hand out
Impulsively looking to the sky for an answer,

There it was,

Three mosquitoes from three directions all casually bounce around in her air
To find a place to quietly land
On her palm
And there they stay unworried, undisturbed

And Gabriela sees their party among thousands was watched by one,
A lone bird, almost waiting for the air to clear somewhere
And for three treats to be so placed inside it
This aura is safe from the weapons that threaten it
Still staring,
Wide-eyed and excited, she sees the bird swoop low,
Closer, up and then slowly down
Right at her palm, and swallow all three
For an instant it lands on her shoulder,
And flees

The men were baffled, useless weapons in the air

How did you do that?

And so she passed them.

The Balance*

When energy is exerted it is also inverted to Balance at the Center with whatever it might encounter.

Feli and Victoria have spread word through the lands
The people of Southland and Northland are deceived
Join, for the Victors are in power,
And their end is near.
Feli has already arranged messengers
Bearing also a word of hope,
Directly from the Writings, "Goodness sleeps"

Thirteen dominant Generations
Through arts of deception and non-involvement
Raising a world of slaves

Power was, is, and will be in the control of those who have seized, are seizing, and will seize it.*

Many were quick on the ball to imitate the Victor's spacetime-proof strategy, and it worked so well that 95% of all quarter-wit or greater species, including those of Earth, waged entirely self-destructive civil wars upon themselves. Entirety, respectfully, has learned from the Victors that nothing else touches the importance of this control, and that those who do not seize it surrender it to someone else. This has proven, is proving, and will prove to be both the most peaceful and destructive Truth in all Truths.

Explosion

Behind the closed door
Of an impenetrably sealed spacecraft
Deafening sounds of rock and metal against metal
Cries and shouts and screaming tones of panic
All were in mortal pain of betrayal
Singing and fighting desperately
It echoed horribly in the underground
The cavern walls ringing back the same agonizing tune
Everyone calling for help
No one listening
And above stomped the footsteps
Of hundreds of thousands charging
Of war breaking out above ground
More misery panging through the dirt ceiling
And much closer
Nearly far too proximal
Came clamoring the climbing noncivilians
Rounding themselves up to the top of the spacecraft
Some merely took assault on the ship
More others took rocks to each other
Continuing man's madness on top of their demise

It was violently real
The volume of my sweat splashing strangers
And the thickness of enemy blood dripping from my wrists
My family is dying in front of me
And I shall follow appropriately
By the hands of a stranger, as I am a stranger
Destroying in all of the confusion around me
In this confusing world I will be destroyed
And it will bring me due clarity

Acid rain usually reserved for the congested energy of deep West Southland
Thundered from the clouds that followed millions
Millions now trying to find something up from the Center
Heavy activity attracting calamity
The greatest force to ever accumulate
Brought forth a third quake, brought forth the explosion
Of its extinction

Abyss

Rise Above

Inside the mysterious metal in the sunken-in Center
Elle, curious
Or possibly hopeful, or, trapped, possibly
In a great dangerous blackness
Impenetrable to the most forceful energies
By all means strengthened by them
From the interior view, along the innocent corridors
Illinut fires in boxes of glass,
Breaking the darkness to and fro
Walls lined with large lidded crates
Filled with seeds of every size and color,
Various stashes of vines, branches, stems, roots, fruits, berries, oats, nectar, and weeds
As if for a group of people for a short amount of time or only a few people for quite a long time, but
Certainly, with all of these boxes of everything, there was only comfortably room for about four

Energy congregated
And the great Western Slope
Erupted like a volcano
Discharging the ship into everything,
Or, nothingness.

Beyond

This realm, there was no light, yet no darkness
Neither black nor white shone, a colorless gray area
In zero gravity, as if this realm were space itself
Or outside of it
There was no echo
No up, down, left, right, or sideways
No sense of space, of place, of time
Nothing in or of the realm itself
For the realm was nothingness
A new reality

They were not taken to a hazy state like that of the Dream plant
This sense was sharper and more direct than sight
And for Elle, more controllable,
Comfortable.

A meaningless purpose,
There is nothing for it.
The words, they will never come, for they do not exist!
What I mean to!
I cannot say it!
This is surely Everything.

Elle was astounded.

Eddy was dumbfounded.

Who are you?

You Know who I am.

There was a vague possibility, most likely made up by Elle's elusive memories

She maybe recollected the voice.

Where am I?

Seemed a relevant question.

The figure with whom she was communicating with seemed to feel at home,

And Elle understood, she already Knew.

Is this what the Victors were doing?
Building a machine to cheat time?

Those inside of it cannot cheat time
They were building a machine to escape
They knew of deep Powers

Verity's voice was faded in whatever separated them

But her tones were powerful and deep

Unlike anything Elle might recall but from a dream

How did she Know all of these answers?
Why did she answer?

To these thoughts Verity had no response

Simply an actual-less energy between them suggested their unimportance

Gabriela shifted her approach

And she tried receiving different answers

Apparently unconcerned of any else

Why am I here?

You were meant to come.

Have I not chosen my own way?

A force always runs north, and south
That brings us where we are meant
There is Balance
As Evil gets worse, Good gets better
As civilizations crumble, new beginnings are made
You walk your own path, and it is of destiny.

What must I do,
With endless time, Knowledge,
Everything,
Experience all existences?

And the nonexistent as well,
If you wish.
You do as you please
But you are meant to exist, Elle
It is your nature
And you may find throughout eternity
Nothing else could be so fulfilling for you
Take your everlasting being and be anything
Do as you guide yourself to
Let not this curse eternally waste you
Let it bless you for all that is Good

And if I desire none of this?

You desire everything, Elle
Let you never be a fool to the contrary

Sadness is a madness
Happiness is for a fool
Balance is an imbalance
To find zen is nearly impossible
And must be, to sustain for eternity

What experience would it be if not to quest for it?
You have everything to lose,
And everything to gain!
Find yourself, everywhere
Be with it
Be your own spirit's guide
For a time will come
When followers follow
To the depths of hell
Through the gates and into fire
And one whom is one with the Goodness in herself
A one that might be so inclined to find her own pathway
She shall see heaven and all its glory
Though herself
There is no adversary,
Nothing to challenge
A neutral being remains eternally
Undriven by lust, luxuries, or thirst
Guide your spirit,
Through and past the end.

How do I begin?

How?
You create your own reality,
You must already Know.

Edward proposed his first inquiry

Am I dreaming?

Yes, I told him.

With couth she pulls Eddy from his state
Elle adapted them into forms
To communicate nothing but a watery stare and final embrace
When she pulled away Eddy was gone.

He awoke with the great first quake.

Eddy's End

Leaving her is beyond regretful
Alone in the endlessness
But this was my dream
And I am unworthy to escape my loop
I am miraculously unfit for infinity,
A journey which I could never fully trespass,
Her presence
And the expanses of time, space, and being; too rich for me
For my life with her has come to its latest
This earned time's spent
I must forfeit undeserved Knowledge
My purpose is to wake Her up
And I must have known it,
Must have believed it,
Just as since my actions proved.
The vastness around my current state mocks my fate
And now, here; apart
I wrap my heart around my body
And return to the world, with reason to wake up from my dream
So that I may wake Her up from Hers
And I regret to leave Her now with such Knowledge
But She must be without me
And I must be for Her.

An Account of Feli

We gravitated together, to the platform atop the central energy. There was Power growing over the spaceship. Stopping ten feet short of the Center, the four of us looked at each other. For a moment no one spoke. I was deathly afraid. A dark shade clouded the area surrounding my brothers who now stood across from each other with dangerous energies. My sister had come from the East and I the West; darting anxious glances at each other and our kin. There was magma bubbling below, rising. The brew to the storm, our special ingredient, was pushing forces. There was Power growing under the spaceship.

"Have you all betrayed me?" Victor articulated weakly.

"No, Victor," called my sister, "Please understand, please, Victor."

He addressed her first. "I understand our purpose. We are all here because of it. Get in the spaceship, Victoria."

"No, Victor." She said it without longing that time.

"We must..."

"No, Victor! We don't need to be parents of a new civilization, we don't deserve any more than these slaves that built this for us."

"We've not enough resources for more than us four for the time it takes to wait out the destruction and feed while the planet remanifests the ripe fungus!"

"Do you intend we play this spin game forever? There must have been an original beginning, not just the most recent one.... Maybe we should change the way beginnings are made?"

"How can we, how do you suggest we do this!?"

"It's much too late, obviously, Victor, for us to decide."

"So why are we not ON THE SHIP?"

"I can't let this happen again!" Our eldest brother was becoming enraged at Victoria's opposition. "We can't!"

"We have to!"

"No we don't! We can end it, now!"

"But our legend will be erased!"

"YES, it WILL! Don't you see? That's what Vittorio wants! We don't NEED to sheppard in a new civilization. We can die, we can finish, and life will figure out a way on Her own...."

At the mention of Vittorio's name the attention of His presence seemed to stir Victor. His face grew redder and he tried to look at Victoria or else glance desperately to me instead of the flesh directly in front of him.

"This is madness! Our Family has been destined to live on, and repeat!"

"Our legacy IS madness, Victor! And I can't doom this fate upon another; let them find existence without me. I'm out!" It was finally Victoria's position. After nights of fighting and denying a predetermined life, She had taken control of Her independence.

"They are an adapted species beyond wildest dreams. How, possibly, could our ancestors have victimized a majority, and left us with the same dirty burden?"

"They were afraid," scorned Vittorio. It was the first I'd heard Him speak in days.

My oldest brother's confidence was shaking. Vittorio was strong having mine and Victoria's energy with His. Victor reverted to defensive tactics. He puffed up his chest, continuing at Victoria. "We are a prideful, wholesome family. We deserve this great destiny. The descendants our ancestors cast aside became so overpopulated, most are irrelevant. They've grown into systematic loops; malfunction-prone and purposeless."

"Independent, and purposeless for you, Victor," Vittorio interjected again.

"Exactly." Finally they looked at each other, and nothing else mattered.

"Yet for their own beings they serve a purpose."

"And what purpose is that?"

"Their own."

Victor XIII had to laugh. "They are meaningless, Vittorio! They are weak, and unimportant unless beneficial."

"They benefit themselves. They live their own lives, and you and I are just as meaningless as they are."

"We are intelligent. We have divine right!"

"We are lucky to have such things. You could easily have been born half Brewer or five-thirteenths Mercantile."

"But I am Victor XIII! I am supposed to live out my destiny. We are! It is Written."

"The Writings do not define our destinies, Victor. We can Write whatever we want, or better yet, we can Write nothing, and no longer live as a Family of tyranny! We can die, and end the madness."

"Pull them together, Feli." A sound resonated to ring in my mind. It came from far away, but seemed to be closer to me than my kin. *"Pull them together, they will turn inside-out."*

I watched my brothers; with fleshthirsty faces and long looks of fury; the hate between them danced with a purple cloud of energy. It was not possible for both of them to come out of this alive. Prospects for my sister and I seemed conjointly bleak. Surely Victor could see that now.

"Feli!" I glanced honorably to Vittorio before looking back to address Victor. My eldest brother, who has forever overemphasized Himself and underestimated the Power of everything besides the Family, turned to his last hope: me. He was about to realize that I only kept him close in hopes of ensuring our Family's message does not negatively taint eternal memory.

"I love the Family, Victor. Sacrifice is the right choice for us." His disbelief seemed unshakable in the final hour of this three hundred thirty-third day. "For the sake of redemption."

Air and flesh of my Family's Known universe spiraled closer to the Center, around us, and the ship. Life was on the brink of gratification.

Vittorio jumped first.

A melting pot of our ancestors swallowed Him as if into a time-shaking wormhole of magma. May his soul live on in Good purpose!

Victoria glanced to my brother and I, and then admired at the spectacle around. Nothing was certain; only what she knew she Knew. And this, now, was her purpose.

Victoria jumped second.

Victor pleaded to our grandfathers and me, on his knees as all energy surrounded. "I cannot understand," was his confession, "only believe."

There was nothing left to say. As I let go something pulled me apart, away, inside-out; my mind unsure what might be happening....

It felt like my eyes were abandoning my body, leaving it relinquished, to be swallowed by the Center.

My final memory before being torn from my universe is Victor's physical expression, defeated by Power, conclusively recalled into the heart of ruin.

Waking

Edward Without

He awoke to the footsteps of passerby in the darkness
Muffled words and shuffling movements
And quiet pitter-pattering.
Gabriela was small next to him,
Close,
And cold,
So he hugged her closer with his warmth.
She did not stir.
She did not breathe.
The breaths that raised his chest were heavy and deep.
Her red curly hair was frizzy, unkempt, travel worn
Carelessly hanging in every direction
Over her face and under her face and over Edward's face
And cold to the touch.
Edward curled a lock of it in his fingers
For several moments,
He stared into her.
Tears fell from him.
Gabriela lay delicately, dead motionless
Ever so much more pale than ever before
No air escaped her fragile body.
And in the darkness his eyes were filled with her
And his ears loud to the weary passerby
And his own tongue disturbed by itself,
Tasting the bitter air of the doomed world.
Without Gabriela there could, and would, never be escape
That was all he could remember.

Night had fallen
Edward was filled with an out-less sense of urgency
Directionless energy
He did not yet realize how long he'd slept
Nor if it mattered,
As an air of fault considered him
Massively overwhelming guilty potential
That would eat at him more than his intoxicants
He could not bear to burn her body

The Dream plant crazes him
He has ended her life
This curse I've brought with him
As I escape hell of deep West Southland
He brings hell home, and to her
By whatever means of Evil
His sleeping beauty has been possessed
What demon am I?
To let this horrible fate
After he let her go
She came back to him and I killed her
What demons have I let in?

For a very long time, by him
She did not wake
Fear eating away at the molds of his limbs
While he starved his body in torture
That he should have fated her to this
All her misery he could not negate
Driving her away from his honesty
Into the cruel world
So that she should return to him after all
A new, dangerous him
That would sacrifice her safety
For love, and bliss
And whatever Knowledge that was to be forgotten
Foolish, he was, and always was
Twisting her dry hair, hoping
Anticipating dreadful aftermath of Dreams

No consumption for a stretch
No bloem
The wholesomeness of his own sanity he held of second importance
His health irrelevant until hers may be discerned
Although it was not obvious how he could help

Traveler Shifts

For a time he let her sleep
Hoping she would regain breath on her own
And if she would,
Wishing that her air be grounded;
A mind astray is no mind to follow
The dangers of Dream Plant seemed too horribly fateful to conceive
And as he let her lie
He knew she would never achieve consciousness alone
Part of him has Seen,
And this light flickered inside of him,
That her consciousness is greater
Her meaning is outside the realm of this world
She is Truth

White noise and buzzing throughout the air
Long enough
Was the time Edward left Gabriela in dream
To hear news of the people
"Goodness sleeps," they whispered
"The darkness is eerie;
Fear looms near."
A trickle of rumors of war
He would never feed to her
That was not their fight
The seriousness of the humanoids with this message
Was as eerie as the words
Never had such a tangible thought
Brought tingling feelings to Edward's spine
He must realize what he already Knew
He must wake Gabriela up.

I was afraid to go along at first,

Were his pleas to her body,

Afraid for you
Afraid for me
Afraid I would watch you walk away
Afraid I could not stand it
Letting you go this way
I knew I had a piece of you
This way I knew, thought, dreamed,
You might be inclined to return
I have learned that if you love something,
Let it go.
We had to let each other go
Let us remember the back of our heads for awhile,
I thought,
If I had any hope of bringing you back
For eternity alone
It was this.
Please, come back,

He pleaded,

Elle.

The name she was meant to be called
Grounded her spirit as nothing else could

Elle's Revival

At last
Alone
Free from consequence
Error
Disappointment
By loss of her kin
Her mind
And everything else

As far as I can imagine
Universes fill the skies
Knowledge surpasses infinite
No One could hold onto it
All is broken into pieces
Concepts, thoughts
Moments
A galaxy is massive to me
Full of ideas to explore
One-at-a-time
Forever
Breadth of Universe
Great expanse of reality
Holds all Truth, secrets, memories
It is expandable upon breeding and birth of a new one
Nothing can hold the Universe
Until all holds onto it,
And lets go.

An energy hints that I will meet Verity again
If not very soon, in a similar manner
Her familiarities
Are ones I haven't recognized yet

It is my reality
And eternity is at my will
I am, have been, will always be
Whatever Elle I manifest to See
Any theme I create, or discover, or destroy
If this is death, or a dream

Fin.

Glossary

-Earth Version-

Bloem (bloém, bloom)

Humans as carbon-based life forms are water-dependent, as the people of this world are fungus-dependent. Bloem is alive, essential, and availably growing in any area of the world. Found in patches, people eat bloem constantly, between every other indulgence and more if possible, to sustain their living beings. Without balanced chemical equation, it is ever-changing, ever-evolving, and evolutionarily necessary for the growth of the people. They have no thirst or need to drink, no public access of water, nor any desire thereof; people only need bloem, or its juice, as a basic.

Ingestion of bloem is a different refreshing emotion depending on the evolved genesis of the plant. A person learns, (or remembers, arguably,) the truth, in a new light of sense. These situationally appropriate emotions always existed within the people, and the bloem is a reminder of the capabilities of change. A world revolving around bloem is an ever-changing world.

As this is not of a specific genus, patches of any shape or color, (usually found ripe at three to four inches tall, in many different textures, and with various shades and tints,) all wear individual patterns at close glance, similar to a human fingerprint. Although generally easy to identify, some poisonous plants disguise themselves similarly to what bloem might look like. Ingesting these hazardous plants can be sickening or fatal. If the plants appear to have a common growth pattern at close look then it is not a bloem patch. To distinguish properly one must look for different prints on the growths.

Growth

Writings of the Victor Family purpose that in the most recent beginning of their time-space the inbred Family cast aside the Brewers, Mercantiles, Shelios and Golds. Memories indicate ancient peoples were more in touch with Knowledge than their descending counterparts.

Tales since the most recent beginning of the ancient Brewers, Mercantiles, Shelios and Golds were forgotten, remembered, tainted, maimed, switched, turned, twisted, belittled, perverted, misunderstood and entirely misrepresented as the generations that proceeded them intermixed and changed everything. Possible truths trail through false tales from similar general knowledge. The interbreeds stretched to the edges of the solid and some proceeded on great ships to venture the liquid sea. Over-breeding and overpopulation caused both the cultivation and expansion of this discivilization.

In the most recent beginning, the ancient Brewers, Mercantiles, Shelios and Golds soon dissolved their essences in the fungus around them. Their physical attributes and emotional tendencies changed. Each sought new methods of plant evolution. Nectars and syrups of bark and root and butters and jellies of berry-like fruit were harvested under the light of day by branches, stems, leaves, buds, and seeds; any bite-sized bit would please. Energy evolved.

When energy is exerted it is also inverted to Balance* at the Center with whatever it might encounter.

Day and Night

A giant cloud protects the inhabitants from a view of what sheds light and darkness for equal amounts of time. A day and night sequence on this planet is roughly a year on Earth; a bit under six months for each consecutively. From the Northern Waters and the bottom of eastern Northland can be seen, briefly, a perspective of the unknown capacity of these great shifts. Though few have witnessed this angle of the light shifts, all have heard a version of it through stories. Travelers describe the great land woven into the vast sea as it becomes suddenly ignited, or so suddenly black that even with this wide view it would take a moment for eyes to adjust. Less level-headed men may lose their minds upon display of this proportion. It is dangerous to think too much. The nature of light and darkness is near complete disregard, what with all the cloudiness.

Day comes and goes and comes and goes in just enough time to make one feel they've been waiting forever and the quarry may never rise again. Then there it is: either illumination or an obscuring darkness, fluctuating in the blink of an eye, whether one's ready for it or not. People do not have historic accounts, only stories, and the count of days and nights since the first story had been told was long ago miscalculated by the public, and given up on. Day and night are assumed mere coincidences, unnumbered and insignificant; simply accepted.

Shelio (she-lee-oo)

Relatable to creatures found on Earth, shelio are mammal-like; smaller than a bear and potential to be equally as fierce, with wool as soft as a vicuñas. They've the loyalty and manner of a dog. Bred in farms in the middle of south Southland, this species is used mostly by people as both a trade commodity and for general protection. Sometimes they are used to pull heavy loads, but not overworked. They're frequently supportive of a friend's (usually individual shelio's or person's) best interests and commonly present in exchanges. People's general perception is of an ally with no disrespect. Stories go that in less crowded times people tried to teach shelio more intelligent ways, such as talking, walking upright and building fire, but the creatures seemed completely incapable, undeveloped of essential digits, and lacking of speech tones other than growls. Nevertheless they're eager to help, particularly to those with whom they have had close contact. More stories say that it is possible to gain the trust of a shelio instantly, and also to lose it instantly. Mistreatment or disrespect of shelio, although instances are rare, have been heard to result in disloyalty and vengeance. Perhaps since they are massively outnumbered, it is more likely for a one to fight another shelio than to attack a person, (who might only win if in possession of a weapon) . Unlike people, shelio commonly mate for life. Most cases provide only one offspring per mating season for a shelio couple (twins rare) in the prime years of their life only, which averages out to 2.5 pups per parents. It is averaged that one-fifth die before reproducing so demographically the shelio population remains nearly the same day-to-day. There is said amongst people, also, that the behavior of shelio bred in the "wild" (outside a farm) tend to be more rambunctious and harder to control than ones bred in captivity and are therefore of lesser and higher trade values but there is no undisputed feature of evidence to conclude the validity of that assumption.

Birds

Flying accumulated energy with a wingspan, birds are prey of shelio and people, which results in their near extinction. Through a few generations of breeding, birds fill skies; and duly, finding unclaimed feathers is rare. Memories stipulate them as quite delicious turned over a fire. Defined dominantly by bird wars, the era of the bird was fruitful, destructive, the associatively destructive... People first fought over who would eat the birds, then later quarreled over the outstanding benefit of birds being eaten at all.

Mosquitoes

Mosquito is the collective name for all types of insects. They are rumored to be born independently of fungus, and not bred. According to memory, their population and evolution is increasing by lack of birds. Insects sense fearful energy of irrational people who don't want their bite or sting; mosquitoes are wary of their lives and defensive in these exponentially dangerous situations of phobia.

Cart (An invention, briefly)

First there was built the basic box, to put things in. Then there was built the wheel; a circular device one may set their box on, in order to push or pull quantities of items for trade, instead of carrying everything in a box. Wheels are large and carts narrow to navigate the uneven ground.

Innovation is kept simple; the easier it may be to familiarize with and utilize, the easier it is to teach, and continue. As adaptations differed and separated, common customs thrived in elementariness.

Cafuné (Brazilian/Portuguese)

The act of tenderly running one's fingers through their lover's hair

Made in the USA
Columbia, SC
19 June 2023

17973169R00138